ID0996736

WIVENHOE

Also by Samuel Fisher

The Chameleon

WIVENHOE

SAMUEL FISHER

BAINTE DEN STOC

WITHDRAWN FROM DLR LIBRARIES STOCK

corsair

CORSAIR

First published in the UK in 2022 by Corsair

1 3 5 7 9 10 8 6 4 2

Copyright © 2022, Samuel Fisher

The moral right of the author has been asserted.

*All characters and events in this publication, other than those
clearly in the public domain, are fictitious and any resemblance
to real persons, living or dead, is purely coincidental.*

All rights reserved.

No part of this publication may be reproduced, stored in a
retrieval system, or transmitted, in any form or by any means, without
the prior permission in writing of the publisher, nor be otherwise circulated
in any form of binding or cover other than that in which it is published
and without a similar condition including this condition being
imposed on the subsequent purchaser.

A CIP catalogue record for this book
is available from the British Library.

ISBN: 978-1-4721-5643-3

Printed and bound in Great Britain by
Clays Ltd, Elcograf S.p.A.
Typeset in Dante by M Rules

Papers used by Corsair are from well-managed forests
and other responsible sources.

MIX
Paper from
responsible sources
FSC® C104740
www.fsc.org

Corsair
An imprint of
Little, Brown Book Group
Carmelite House
50 Victoria Embankment
London EC4Y 0DZ

An Hachette UK Company
www.hachette.co.uk

www.littlebrown.co.uk

FOR MY BROTHERS

A not admitting
of the Wound
Until it grew so
wide
That all my
life had entered it

EMILY DICKINSON

JOE

When they arrived at the river, Ian's eyes were still open. A circle of people had gathered a few feet from where the snow had finally staunched the blood. Slightly apart, half-turned, stood Patrick – the axe hanging from his gloved hand.

The ice that clung to Patrick's eyelashes was flushed claret. This garishness – rimming his unseeing eyes, fixed on the ice below – made Joe think of the wooden heads that hung in the rafters of St Mary's: the painted faces of dead aldermen who funded the church's restoration, now watching over their descendants. He thought of the way their rictus and rouged cheeks mocked the solemnity of the place.

Joe had wanted to ask the obvious question. It was on his lips. But for some reason, when he opened his mouth it produced another.

'What have you done?'

Already, instead of causes, his mind was turning to consequences.

Patrick turned his back, raising his hand to shield his eyes from the late sun. The fabric of his hood had crimped and hardened into gentle waves, its stitchwork was coming loose.

Joe heard Ian's mother before he saw her, silhouetted against blue double doors of the Nottage, calling her son's name above the thump of the generator. It gave shape to their days: a din you didn't notice until it stopped.

When he turned back, Patrick was already moving away across the snow. Fleeing the sound of Ian's name.

Joe stood and watched with everyone else as Sandra crossed from the old bank to where they now stood – still – in the middle of the frozen river. He watched as she stumbled. When she finally arrived, she let out a wail with which life resumed. She fell to her knees and all of the women moved towards her, bearing her up.

There was a lull then, as the men loitered watchfully – waiting for someone to do something, to take charge – a stand-off which was broken when Ian's father arrived. Red with drink and cold, Alan took one look at his son and threw up. He grabbed Joe, swore oaths and cursed Patrick's name, but Patrick was already gone.

Joe watched his mother cradle Sandra and tried to remember when he had last seen her out of the house. He tried to remember the last time the whole village had been together like this, gathered in one place. He realised how much their numbers had dwindled. For just a moment, he felt weirdly elated, just to be near to so many people.

Once Sandra and Alan had been half dragged, half carried away, the villagers left in their ones and twos, until only Joe and Alfie remained. They fetched a sled from the Nottage and dragged Ian's body to the quayside. Alfie dug out a tarp. Without any discussion they wrapped the body, Joe's fingers cramping in his mittens, and slid it under the hull of an upturned, abandoned dinghy, weighted by stones to keep the foxes off.

They slumped against the hull of the boat; the light was fading and the generator fell silent. Then, they trudged home and, for the first time in months, Joe sat with Alfie at the kitchen table and drank until the cold left his bones.

*

For the moment, as the blood beats in his tongue, Joe forgets where he is.

His heart slows and it's the distant thump of the generator that recalls the events of the previous day; a sequence of unreal images unfolding against his eyelids. He levers himself out of bed, pulling thermals on with fast, practised movements, before drawing back the curtains.

He winces at the glare. Never thought he would miss the mud: the gleaming slickness of it. The slap and suck at the turning of the tide; its rich, bird-shit stink after a hot day and a couple of pints at the Rose as the sun tickled the clouds pink. The green-blue-yellow hues that marked the changes in the light as the days and seasons marched over the village and the river. And now, just snow. Endless snow.

There was a seal once, before. He had spotted them in the river in the past, but this one was parked up on the mud, right in front of the pub. People were throwing it chips which carved short furrows in the sludge. The seal left them where they lay. Arched its back, nose in the air: not interested. After a couple of minutes, it slipped down the bank back into the river and was gone.

'Joe?'

He lets fall the curtain and the gloom resettles: warmth of the bed, smell of Rachel's breath.

3

'Go back to sleep. Sun is only half up.'

As he pulls on one of his boots, his strength drains. He sees it leave him in the moisture of his breath, which whitens the air. Rachel sighs as she turns in her sleep.

Before yesterday, he had been coming around to the idea that the snow was a good thing. It had thrown them on their own resources. When those who had left, gone off to the city years before for work or university, came back down the train track, arriving with the rest of the sorry lot – down-from-Londons dressed in their fancy down jackets, hungry and cold – he'd felt vindicated.

Maybe Patrick had always had it in him: a latent violence.

He slips his hand under the covers, to find the warm curve of Rachel's backside before coming to rest on her hip. For a second, he considers taking his clothes off again and getting back in with her. But he knows he would regret it later, missing the moments of crisp silence out in the solitude and the biting cold. A well to draw on, when the rest of the day comes, with its demands.

So, he pulls on his other boot and trudges down the stairs. In the kitchen he opens and closes cupboards. Though he knows what he will find, he has a notion that a fresh orange might have materialised, miraculously, in the night. An orange plump with sunshine that would leave its sharp scent on his fingers as he goes about his day.

The halftracks will be arriving this afternoon. Hunched over the counter, he luxuriates in a moment of self-pity.

He presses a couple of oatcakes into his pocket and gasps as he lets himself out into the cold.

HELEN

When Helen hears the front door close, she gives up on the pretence of sleep.

The idea of packing while her son was still in the house, banging around in the empty cupboards downstairs, had felt like too much of a betrayal.

Now that Joe has gone and she is free to get up, she feels entirely spent. She swings her legs over the side of the bed and rocks back and forth onto her heels. Helen has learned not to trust her body these past months, like the ground beneath her feet has developed a tendency to lurch and roil.

Last night, Bill had told her that he was leaving with Patrick, boldly: bracing for a fight. There was no question of whether Patrick could stay, and Bill couldn't let him go alone. Patrick wouldn't make it onto the boat unless he could pretend to be a carer for his dad. Still no evacuation order for the able-bodied. Bill couldn't conceal his surprise when she said she was coming along too. She looks over at him now – his lips slightly pouted in sleep – and wonders whether he was disappointed. Whether, in his calculation of the future, he had already accounted for losing her. If there is one thing she knows about him, it's that he doesn't like a change of plan. He can be spontaneous, but only under controlled conditions.

She thinks, for some reason, of the first time she met Bill: watching as he pursued a naked, five-year-old Ian around her back garden. Ian had stripped off all his clothes and started chasing the other little boys and girls. Joe's seventh birthday party, on the day that Princess Diana died. Patrick must have been there too, but she can't picture him; his newly divorced dad made a greater impression. It was a sweltering day that ended in a thunderstorm. She remembers making sandwiches with Sandra, packet ham and egg mayonnaise. And that she had cried. It almost makes her laugh to think of it. The absurd anxiety that it had caused, that Diana might have died on Joe's birthday.

That was not so long after her mum died. It was a time in her life when she would seek out mirrors whenever she cried, finding comfort in being a witness to her own grief. A time from which every memory has a strange timeless lucidity.

She cries all the time now and couldn't care less. Things that happened just a couple of days ago are hard to bring to mind, but the further back she goes the clearer things are. She feels like she can pluck days from those years like buttons from a jar, turning them over in her fingers. A different person. A person who was touched by the events occurring around her. Someone who experienced them with such a strength of feeling that she almost blushes to recall.

All of this – she wouldn't mind so much, if not for the pain that follows her around like a wild animal, tensed to pounce.

When she thinks of Ian, lying in the snow, his head split like a windfall apple, she feels nothing. This is why she has to leave.

She wants all of her memories of this place to stay colourfast, untouched by what is happening to her body.

Joe's memory of her too. She wants it unblemished.

Bill stirs and she pats him on the thigh.

'Best be getting up, old man.'

He opens his eyes, a smile forming at the corners of his mouth. Then the previous day's events return to him and the smile evaporates. She wishes for a moment that she had held the axe, to spare him from this.

She pats him on the thigh once more and gets to her feet.

JOE

He pauses at their rotten front gate, a moment of indecision.

Ordinarily, he would turn right and walk along the quay to check that no one had been at the supplies at the Nottage, then cut across the frozen river course to trudge along the opposite bank, before doubling back when he reached the tidal barrier. It still has the air of novelty even after a year: this erosion of boundaries. The way the snow flattens out the landscape.

Today he turns left. He doesn't want to pass the pyre that he and Alfie built last night, after drinking away the cold at the kitchen table, in preparation for today's funeral.

He walks until he reaches the new houses and stops at the base of the big red shed. It stands at the edge of a slight depression in the snow, marking out the location of the small harbour where a few local fishermen used to moor their trawlers. Of all the new housing developments in the village, he finds the conversion of the old shipyard the least offensive. From a distance the apartment building passes for the corrugated-iron-clad shipwright's shed that it replaced. It's the same colour and shape at least. Even if the ramshackle charm of the old place doesn't hold up when the new building – with its plastic cladding and Juliet balconies – is subjected to closer inspection, he feels grateful that some attempt was made to preserve the spirit of what was lost. Now, the ravages of the weather are returning it to that spirit day by day.

Almost everyone who lived in the building, before the snow, has left. The sole occupants are those who set out from the city after it began falling, carried with that great tide of people to the coast, only to wash up here.

Those eligible for evacuation from the village didn't leave all at once. Pregnant women and their partners went first, and then the young families, taking along grandparents where they could. But among the elderly there were some hold-outs: the knackered old sots who had propped up the bar at the pub before it started snowing, gnashing their false teeth and practically foaming at the mouth as they yammered on about fishing quotas and blue passports. The thought that they would have to turn to the object of their barstool sermons for help was too much to countenance. Until it wasn't. And then they were gone too, all aside from Reg.

He feels a sudden and powerful urge to climb. When he thinks of those bitter old cunts he always needs to use his body – to reassure himself with the readiness of his limbs. The exigencies of this new world make it difficult to sustain the adversarial affection he once felt for them.

The wrought iron balconies provide good footing. He can feel himself start to sweat as he pulls himself up from one to the next. After three storeys, he heaves himself over the lip of the slanting roof and lies on his back for a moment to catch his breath, before he shimmies upwards on his belly, enjoying the protective feeling of his snowsuit against the fresh snow crunching underneath him.

He straddles the apex and turns towards the sea. Casting his eyes along the course of the river towards the estuary, the bleached landscape bleeds into the sky; he raises his gaze, momentarily catching a hold of towering clouds the colour of a young gull's wings, before dropping his eyes down in search of an interruption. The horizon eludes him again. Without a sense of depth or distance he feels dizzy and presses his eyes closed. More and more often lately, he has felt that it is time to pack up and leave. But every time he comes back to this spot, he knows he can't. There's still the chance that the snow could stop falling, that it could melt and give him back his home.

They had been talking about having a baby, he and Rachel. He had never felt the urge until the snow. It offers some sense of future: a handhold to shift this suspended time. Just need to get through today, to be ready for when the shipment arrives. Then there will be some time to think.

He hears someone approaching – the lisping sound of boots on the freshly fallen snow. He scoots down to the edge of the roof and sees Alfie, a spade under his arm.

'Alright, mate,' he calls up. 'Thought I might find you here.'

Joe clambers down the side of the building. He can hear Alfie humming 'Winter Wonderland'. Daft cunt is always humming that tune, no matter what time of year. In moments of absent-mindedness, or when he's concentrating. Or when there is something unsaid, in the air between them. In moments when humming a tune is a way of saying it while leaving it unsaid.

They walk together to the tidal barrier, clambering over the top few feet of gate that remain, forlorn and futile, above the snowline. It's not until they're sat atop the barrier that he feels safe to open his mouth.

'What was your excuse? For slipping out.'

'I told Mum I was off down the Nottage. Dig the entryway out. Turn the snow over. Get rid of the blood before it freezes hard under the new snowfall. Get a headstart. There's hardly going to be a spare fucking minute today, after all.'

'After all.'

Alfie holds up his spade and makes the sign of the cross in the air.

'Remember when we found Ian in the drum of that concrete mixer, over by the pits?'

Joe sighs. Alfie doesn't hear him, or pretends not to.

'You know. In the junkyard. Over by the old pits, the ones that got filled in?'

'Yes, mate. I remember.' Joe speaks just to shut him up, but regrets the edge in his voice. One summer, when they were around ten or so, they would steal tyres from that scrapyard by the pits and roll them down the hill into the lake. They both loved to watch as the tyres cut a drunken path through the rushes before sinking below the surface of the water with an almighty splash. It was even better when there were a couple of rusty old bastards snoozing by their fishing rods who would jump up, spluttering and cursing, while Joe and Alfie remained hidden out of sight, cackling and punching one another in the arm, trying to make the other cry out.

'He was just sitting in there, on his own,' Alfie says.

'Yeh. In the dark.'

'Throwing stones against the inside of the mixer.'

'And do you remember—'

'When that bloke came along? I remember.'

Ian had given them the fright of their lives, when he poked

11

his head out of the mouth of that ruined concrete mixer. He climbed down, dirt all over his tracksuit bottoms, and they asked him what he was doing. He held out a handful of pebbles, as though that were an explanation.

As they were leaving the scrapheap a man appeared, walking the road from the diggers back to the Portakabins where they kept their lunches. A worker from the pits. They all ducked down to hide, Ian lagging slightly behind. As the man passed them on the road Ian, for whatever reason, threw a pebble at the barrel that Joe and Alfie were hiding behind. The worker paused and then turned to investigate the sound. Just as he was about to reach Joe and Alfie's hiding place Ian jumped up and started yelling.

'What was it he called the bloke?' Joe says.

'A paedo.'

'A fat, dirty paedo.'

'That was it.'

Alfie starts up with 'Winter Wonderland' again.

'He always was a bit of an arsehole,' Alfie says, 'wasn't he?'

'Yeh. He was. Whatever that tells us.'

'You're right. There were worse.'

They stand for a moment in silence; the gentle din of the generator is brought to them on the breeze.

'Time to put that spade to some use?' Joe says.

Alfie raises it in the air like a sword and as he does, he says, 'To the Nottage!'

HELEN

She looks up and Bill is there in front of her. She can tell by the look on his face – something finely balanced between concern and frustration – that this isn't the first time that he has called her name.

'Helen. Do you need anything else?'

She looks over at the bags he has packed, waiting by their bedroom door.

'Do you need to bring anything else?'

She smiles and watches him soften. This, she can still achieve. He gets up, his knees cracking, and sits down beside her.

'Did you hear her last night?' he says.

'Who?'

'Sandra. She was banging on the windows. Screaming and yelling. Throwing things. Shouting for Patrick to come out.'

Patrick wasn't in the house; Helen knew that much. When Bill heard what happened he packed a few things in a bag, and sent him off to Bowyer's farm down the creek with Naomi, to spend the night out of harm's way. She has no memory of hearing Sandra. To think of her screaming only summons the image of her eighteenth birthday, sprinting together across the playing fields down toward the pub in the pissing rain. Can that really have been over thirty years ago? To think of her tearing at her hair, as she had been on the river yesterday, is somehow absurd.

'Did you go out to her?' she says.

'No. Eventually she left. It was heavy last night. It will make things tough-going today. Where is Joe?'

'I heard him go out earlier on. He'll be back soon.'

'What will you tell him?'

'Nothing.'

Bill turns his head towards her and begins to try to find words. She takes her hand away and cuts him off before he has the chance.

'You'll say nothing to him either. It's better this way.'

He opens his mouth again but she pulls him towards her, touching his forehead to hers. She's always loved this bluster, the am-dram patter of their relationship. It's a comfort now. He'll always question her, but only to draw an affirmation that she is doing what she wants. Like a whetstone. Does she want this? Yes. Does she really want to leave her son? Yes. She sees herself, for a moment, sitting on the bed next to Bill, reciting Catechism, not that she has ever for a moment been a Catholic but she has read a few Edna O'Brien novels. She could be an Irish heroine, long-suffering and harbouring a terrible secret. She certainly suffers. She feels she needs to tell herself over and over, in her head: I'm leaving. To prevent herself from blurting it out in the kitchen, when Joe gets home. I'm leaving. I'm leaving. It's an incantation and – just as whenever she is touched by a feeling that borders on the religious – she repeats it with a sense of shame. As she repeats it to herself she simulates the moment that she and Joe will meet downstairs, in just a minute, in all of its many iterations because despite the shame – inside of it – there is a feeling of safety; this impossible loop in which she is leaving but also meeting Joe again and again, for the last time, and never leaving.

'Helen?'

Bill's look tells her, again, that it's not the first time he has said her name.

'Did Patrick say anything to you, about what he was going to do?'

The question takes her by surprise.

'No, he didn't. You?'

'No. He was angry. Furious. But he didn't say he was going to go off and do something like this.'

They sit together, for a moment. Helen knows what Bill needs to hear. The shame, and the safety inside of it.

'He didn't say anything, but I suppose that I knew. Knew that he might.'

'Yes. I suppose I did too.'

He squeezes her hand and holds it for a few moments too long for it to be a gesture of reassurance, until it spills over into quiet desperation.

'My stupid boy. What am I going to do with him.'

Helen squeezes back.

'We'll be alright.'

As she says these words she feels the circumscribed truth of them. With it, a flood of relief. It's enough.

Bill opens his mouth to say something else but as he does Helen hears the front door open and thud close and his words wash over her.

JOE

When they arrive at the Nottage the snow has already been shovelled; the fresh, white powder heaped on top of the old to create a ravine leading up to the ramp. There are two pairs of snowshoes hanging on the hooks by the double doors.

Joe casts a look at Alfie. He feels a sudden nervousness as to who they might find inside. So close to the generator, conversation is impossible. They take off their snowshoes, hang them with the others and head through the double doors.

He is relieved to find that it's just the vicar and Reg. He smiles to himself as he thinks it's the first time he's been relieved to see that old git's face.

'Why aye, man,' Reg says, turning from his position by the oil radiator. 'Surprised to see you showing your face this morning.'

'Don't start, Reg. Not today,' the vicar says, as he struggles to right the hull of an upturned, half-finished clinker dinghy. Joe rushes to help him but arrives a moment too late and the boat crashes to the floor, making a shockingly loud sound in the enclosed space.

They stand in silence as it rocks to stillness.

'Don't know what you'd have a right to be smirking about,' Reg mutters to himself, 'gone bloody daft, lad.'

'I thought we could use this as a potato store,' the vicar says. 'If any arrive today. The cold got to the last lot.'

'I used to have one of these,' Joe says. He runs his hand along one of the exposed ribs. His mum had paid for Bill to do one of the boatbuilding courses that they ran here one year. It coincided with the first time Joe read *Swallows and Amazons*, so he and Patrick spent a summer rowing the boat that Bill had built up and down the river, flying the skull and crossbones. The closest they came to privateering was yelling obscenities at the old hermit who lived in the broken-down houseboat, up the creek. By the next summer it was forgotten. His mum donated the boat to a pub at the top of the village and they turned it into a planter.

'Morning, Vicar,' Alfie says, as he passes into the back, waving his phone. 'Gonna get some juice.'

'Morning, Alfie.' The vicar raps a knuckle against the wood. 'Yes, this one seems to have been forgotten, Joe. I dragged it out from behind some plastic crates. I wish I had taken hold of this place right at the start, before it was overrun by bored kids waiting to be evacuated. Might have saved more.'

He gestures at the walls, at the remains of the maritime exhibits that made up the Nottage's collection. Half models of boats built in the village, watercolours of the finished products cutting through white tops around the world. A sextant lies on its side in an otherwise empty glass case.

A portrait of a group of men shows a yachting crew from the turn of the last century, decked out in matching uniforms. From the description Joe deduces that the extravagantly moustachioed man standing at the centre is Captain Charles Nottage.

It's a comically masculine scene; he can almost smell the pipe smoke and leather.

'What do you think, Vicar?' Joe says. 'Do you reckon this lot would have made a better go of it than us?'

The vicar approaches and studies the photograph. 'If those moustaches are anything to go by—'

'Where's that brother of yours, Joe?' Reg interrupts.

'Leave *off*, would you, Reg?' the vicar says. 'For pity's sake.'

He holds his hands up. 'I don't blame the lad. That Ian were always a wrong'un. Touched.'

The vicar lowers his voice. 'How are you holding up, Joe?'

Joe grimaces. What is there to be said?

'Would have done the same meself, truth be told,' Reg breaks in again. 'If what is said is true. Would have done the same.'

'And what the fuck would you know about it, Reg? Haven't you got somewhere else to be?' Joe barks. The vicar places a hand on his shoulder and Joe takes a deep breath, trying to take hold of himself.

Reg raises his hands once more, and shakes his head – the voice of reason, shunned. 'All's else I'll say is that if tha lad has any sense he'll not show his face. He'll have to answer for it. He'll have to answer for what he's done.' He gets up and staggers over to the stairs.

'Ignore him, Joe. He's drunk.'

'Already?'

'What happened yesterday has put a lot of strain on everybody.'

When the snow started falling, Joe was drinking a lot. Every day. They all were, in a frenzied state of festivity. Still plenty on the shelves then, unless you wanted chickpeas. For some reason that seemed to be a hoarder's favourite – check the cupboards of the kitchen in any abandoned house and you'll find stacks of them. And there was power all day. He and Rachel cooked elaborate meals for Bill and his mum, recipes that called for rose petals. He even took to smoking meat in the Weber, out in the back garden.

Then he and Alfie got into brewing beer as something to do. When they decided to turn the Nottage into a community centre of sorts, somewhere to store the supplies that were being sent across the Channel, they took it a step further and built a still out of an old pressure cooker. When they couldn't get grain any more they used the potatoes and canned sweetcorn coming in each week to make a mash.

Then they set up a bar upstairs. Fancied themselves owners of a frontier saloon; serving shine at the trading post. It was fun, until it got old. There's only so many times you can talk about the weather with the same people, when it never changes. Their clientele thinned as more and more people started to leave for the Continent. Joe grew sick of the same old faces, sick of never having anything to report. He started staying away; left it to Alfie.

Finally Reg took over the still. Ostensibly, what he produced was for the community, but even if anyone was able to get their hands on it before he poured it down his miserable gullet, there was no one lining up. He took less care than Joe and Alfie had. The general feeling was that the risk of going blind from his gut-rot brew, on top of everything else, wasn't worth the pleasant effects.

He can hear Reg mithering, Alfie snapping at him.

'You've got the patience of a saint, Vicar. Putting up with that sorry old bastard every day.'

'Patrick came to see me,' the vicar says, 'a few days ago.'

'Did he? Did he tell you he was going to . . .' Joe trails off. 'Did he tell you what he had planned?'

'Do you think if he had told me that I would have let him go back out into the village?' The vicar picks up one of the plastic crates, knocked on its side by the boat. He begins to stack them. 'I don't know what I would have done. But no, he didn't tell me.'

'What did he want then?' Joe says. 'A quick lesson in the scripture?'

'Don't be cruel, Joe. Just because it means nothing to you doesn't mean that—'

'I know. I'm sorry.'

'He was upset. But he was circumspect, and I was distracted. To be honest, I didn't think much of it at the time. Lots of people are coming to me, acting strangely. People who showed no interest before, either in me or the church.'

'What did you say to him?'

'I don't know – what I always say. I can't remember. I feel responsible. I just wish that he'd said more.'

'It's not your fault, Vicar. Not everything is your fault.'

'I've spent my whole life here, in the village, listening to people's problems. Petty miseries and heartbreaks, all of which would, in all probability, have solved themselves without the benefit of my soothing words. And Patrick came to me with this murderous rage in his heart. Here I was. Worrying about frozen potatoes.'

'It's not your fault.'

'I just wish that I had paid more attention.'

'Yeh. I think we all wish we paid more attention.'

20

Joe picks up the last crate and stacks it on top of the rest. The Nottage is clean and tidy, ready for the arrival of supplies.

'What will you do, Vicar? When the halftracks arrive. Will you tell them?'

'Reg was right about that, at least. Patrick is going to have to answer for what he did.'

Joe opens his mouth to ask the vicar what exactly he means by this when Alfie thunders down the stairs. He does a clowning double take: Joe to the vicar, and then back again.

'Oh, I'm sorry. Did I interrupt a heart-to-heart?'

The change of tone is abrupt; the vicar turns away to the corner, where he picks up a broom. Joe laughs and tells Alfie to fuck off, because what other response is there? He feels a tightness in his chest – the spectre of anxiety – and pumps his fists to get the blood moving. He tunes into the thump of the generator and for a moment it seems synchronous with the blood in his ears. It is a momentary, uncanny feeling. As he straightens up, it passes.

He has had an anxiety attack only once, getting the tube back to Liverpool Street after a night on the gear with some of the lads who were living down there. It was early. He wanted to get the first off-peak train so he could spend the day lying in bed. He had a seat but still had the feeling he needed to sit down. It was a hammer-heart swell and crash; the inside of a wave, watching the world down its barrel. And cold sweat, teasing the hairs on the back of his neck. When he got off at Liverpool Street, bundling his way up the escalator, out into the cavernous station, it passed. By the time he got home it was forgotten.

He has felt that wave cresting these past few months.

'Had any grockles through here past couple of days?' Alfie asks.

'Thankfully not,' says the vicar. 'I wouldn't have much to offer them.' He holds his hands wide, the broom in the crook of his elbow.

It had started as a private joke between Joe and Alfie, calling them grockles, these people who passed through the village, flowing from the city to the coast. They had been to a houseparty once out on Mersea Island, when they were still in college. Joe had just got his first car and they were making the most of it: gatecrashing parties all over the county thrown by friends of friends when their parents were out, and then sleeping on reclining seats until they could convince themselves that Joe was safe to drive. This particular party had gone south. Someone had put their foot through the glass dining table and the host was inconsolable. Her boyfriend (older) started waving a baseball bat around, sending them scuttling out the door. When they woke, they discovered someone had written FUCK OFF GROCKLES in the dust on the bonnet of the car. For some reason, they found this unbearably funny.

Whenever one of these travellers passed though the Nottage, after they had been fed and watered, Joe and Alfie would mime ringing a bell and chirp the phrase at one another in an exaggerated estuary accent. Somehow, everyone else caught on. At first Joe was embarrassed, because stripped of its context, it wasn't really funny at all. Irony was a flimsy defence; he felt guilty that he had brought something so ungenerous into their everyday speech. But after a while – as with so many of the changes and accommodations of the last twelve months – it became so commonplace that he didn't think about it anymore.

They zip up their snowsuits. Alfie is out the door and Joe is about to follow when the vicar calls his name.

'Mind you keep Patrick away from Alan today.'

'I'll try.'

As they walk along the quay, Joe spots a curtain twitch. A figure in the window, their face obscured.

'Whose house is that?' he asks Alfie.

'I thought Dennis lived there? Was that his name? The one with the limp.'

'He left.'

'Fuck knows, then. Bet they're loving this, though. Most excitement they've had in an age.' Alfie bends down and forms a snowball, lobbing it up at the window, where it flattens against the pane. The curtain twitches closed. 'Nosy old fucks.'

Joe looks out across the river. He can hardly blame them.

They're almost at Joe's gate now, and they slow. Joe is in no rush to go back inside, to start the day proper. Alfie squats for a moment in the snow.

'Joe, did Patrick say anything to you? About Ian.'

'Not since Naomi spoke to him. I did hear him the night before last. He came late. Speaking quietly with his dad.'

Alfie spits in the snow.

When he heard Patrick arrive he had almost gone down. The prelude to real violence is not shouting and screaming, but something low and musical; the tension coiled in the belly. When Patrick left he felt a powerful urge to open the window and shout down to him, but suppressed it. Instead, he watched him walk away and knew that he could unwind that coil in Patrick, if he had wanted. He had not come to his father to be talked down. He came for his anger to be witnessed. So that afterwards, his dad could say to himself: that's why.

'Better go in,' Joe says.

Alfie gets to his feet. 'We're going to have to have a word with Sandra, aren't we? About the funeral.'

'Thinking the same thing. I'll knock for you and we can go over together. After breakfast.'

'Right you are. In a bit then, mate.'

'Yeh.'

Joe watches for a moment, as Alfie moves over the snow, until he reaches the cut that leads off the quay towards the high street. Then he turns and heads inside.

HELEN

She needs a moment to take stock. She has always been a bad actress but recently she has grown more skilled at impersonating herself. Pain is a quick teacher.

She takes the bags from their place by the door and kicks them under the bed. Not that Joe will come into her room, hasn't done in years. But it's part of the act: mother that remains.

She checks her face in the mirror over her dressing table. Her second self tickles her skin, making her hair stand up on end. Time to go downstairs.

Joe is leaning against the countertop, still wearing his coat, gloves off, drumming his fingers on the Formica. Bill is rinsing their tea mugs from the previous night. They have a silent readiness that makes Helen feel like they are waiting for the audience lights to go down. Waiting for her so that they might speak.

She takes her seat. She tries out a few questions in her head. Rachel still asleep? Had something to eat? By the time she cycles around to the third – much new snow on the ground? – she realises that not having managed to say the first thing that came to her, by beginning the conversation without Joe (yes, sheltering in the branching tree of all those possible iterations, which was a solace when she was alone), she has stalled it. She has silenced herself. When Joe was two or three there was a period when he would respond to anything that she said with the question: why? An idle enquiry that would build to a furious demand for her to break the circular logic of her justifications, to get to the root of the thing. That she simply didn't know was never satisfactory. The fact that she couldn't explain why the sky was blue was as unacceptable as being unable to tell him why he had to hold his knife and fork a certain way. Physical phenomena were of a piece with that other unfathomable thing: her motives. His repeated question became a demand: know yourself! She felt so powerful, to be the guardian of his reality, and yet so powerless to hold anything in place. She can't remember who she was before she became his mother; before she was remodelled in the cleaving light and shade of Joe's ceaseless demands.

'You alright, Mum?' he asks.

A half-eaten oatcake hovers by his mouth and she doesn't know how much time might have passed while she has been sitting there, waiting to begin. Her face feels flushed. The gas heater is alight in the corner. She hopes that more canisters arrive today; that must be the last one. They've restricted themselves to two hours a day, one in the morning, one in the evening.

'Have you been out this morning, then?' She takes a seat at the table and a nerve twangs like a frayed string, sending a disordered flash of pain up the back of her left leg. She attempts to divert the grimace into a smile.

'Yeh, just went to clear my head, clear some snow from the Nottage. Bumped into Alfie. He'd had the same idea.'

'Who was there?' Bill asks.

'The vicar. Reg.'

She always knows the shape of his days now, as she did when he was a child. There were years when she wouldn't see him for days. But there is no work now and, lately, people drink their moonshine at home. She wonders whether he finds it claustrophobic, this regression, in the way that she does. She could never ask him; he would just laugh it off. The old stoic act. He gives her the details of his day-to-day life as a defence – who he has passed on the quay, what small jobs he has done around the Nottage – to bring her close enough to hold her at arm's length. It's not healthy for him to have so little to do.

It was only a matter of time before something happened. The snow's silence has thrown everyone in on one another. When Patrick left the house the night before last he was practically breathing fire. They should have realised that he needed to be talked away from the ledge. To be told that he was wrong, to have his fury triggered by counterargument, so that it might spill out harmlessly and expend itself before it reached its target.

'How are you bearing up?' she asks.

'Still breathing.'

Bill looks reproachfully over his shoulder at Joe, from his position by the sink.

'In the circumstances . . .' she says.

'Sorry.'

'It's OK.'

'Don't know what to do with myself. Best get it out of my system before I go and see Sandra about the funeral. Need to do it today. The foxes.'

'Have you had anything to eat? Other than that oatcake?'

'Where's Patrick?' he says, looking down at his nails.

27

Bill is polishing the same glass over and over. She knows where Patrick is. But she knows in the context of her leaving. She feels her mounting silence, rising between her and Joe. She needed something to change, to draw her away. And she could believe it of Ian. You're not supposed to think this of children, but even as a boy she saw a cruelty in him. There was something out of step. His father had a streak of it: stupidity that was as hard as old rope. Alan made her feel like a snob, simply being in his presence. The thought of rope now recalls his calloused fingers and the time that she kissed him – a version of herself – or, rather, that she allowed herself to be kissed. He pursued her and she relented because Sandra was interested in him and she wondered if she might be too. A couple of weeks before her eighteenth birthday. It's hard to believe: his clumsy hands, his bloodless lips.

She needs to say something. Again, that urge to laugh aloud and with it a feeling of how tentative her grip is, of how easy it might be to drift away.

'Let me make some pancakes,' Bill finally says. 'We need something hot to eat. Still a little flour left.'

He busies himself with the flour, milk powder, water and whisk. More gas, then. She supposes it doesn't matter but she can't break the habit of mentally inventorying.

'I better wake Rachel,' Joe says. 'She'll go nuts if she finds out she's missed pancakes.'

He shuffles out into the hall, pulling off his coat.

As Bill drops the first ladleful of batter in the pan he starts to sing 'Moon River'. He has a lovely tenor, like warm honey. He smiles at her and she marvels at his ability to arrange this moment. Joe is going to see Sandra. This fact has only just registered itself.

'I think I'll go along with Joe,' she says.

Bill stops singing. 'Hmm?'

'I think I'll go with Joe, to see Sandra.'

He puts down the spatula and turns his body towards her, folding his arms. He studies her for a second. 'Do you think that's a good idea?'

'I'll just go along with him, that's all. Offer some comfort.'

'I told Patrick we would go and check in on him this afternoon. That we would be ready to leave by the evening,' he says, lowering his voice.

She feels compelled to put herself before Sandra, to see what happens. A residual loyalty which demands she gives herself the opportunity to confess. Or at least to witness her anguish.

'I have to go along. It wouldn't be right.'

Joe had been on the cusp of moving out when the snow started; he and Rachel were in the process of buying a place of their own. They had been considering the new builds on the edge of town. But it makes no sense to live apart now. Staying together makes food and fuel stretch a little further. Makes her feel glad, though she knows Joe would like a bit more space. Rachel had moved in here when her parents upped and left their house, a two up two down on the high street. Only people in those new builds now are the grockles who've come down the railway line.

Joe and Rachel sit down to eat. Bill puts the plate of steaming pancakes in the middle of the table alongside the little bowl of sugar and the bottle of Jif. What she would give for a real lemon.

JOE

Joe hangs his coat in the hall and climbs the stairs, enjoying the give of the wood. He is grateful for the supple familiarity of this old house.

He has noticed a growing slowness about his mother in the last few months. It comes and goes: a tendency to pause in doorways, chin slightly raised, as though listening out for some signal no one else can perceive. And the silences, from which she returns not with wry insight, but a refiguring of a question which she asked fifteen seconds before. He can't pinpoint the moment when clarity came to be the surprise, rather than its opposite. Which is how it always is: the scale tips so slowly you only notice when the weight is lifted and it tips back. He tries to think back to how she was before the snow, after all it's less than a year, but the days are too slippery to nock against. The arrow slips.

He doesn't ask, or call her attention to it. No one asks. Not in a way that invites a response outside of the expected platitudes.

Easy conversation is now impossible because at any moment she might withdraw to that other, unreachable place. Joe grows frustrated by his own lack of patience and begins to feel like he's losing control of what might come out of his mouth. There's only so long he can stand it – her mirror-lake stillness – before he has to toss a pebble to see the surface ripple. When she asked him how he was in the kitchen just now, he almost answered honestly; that one part of him is glad Ian is dead and another wishes he had never been born, that he and Rachel had fucked last night, after everything, as if they might never see each other again, with what felt like a single breath held between them. Pink of his fingertips pressing white haloes into her thighs, her arms. The soles of her feet, afterwards, reflected in the mirror, silvery in the moonlight. They had fallen asleep without a word.

He's about to go into their room when he notices that the door to Patrick's room is ajar. He pulls it closed and, as he does, sees that all of Patrick's drawers have been pulled open. He didn't take much with him.

Rachel is still fast asleep. He opens the curtains but she doesn't stir – her back to him, facing the wall. The snow has made them apathetic. He remembers the day he realised that there would be no more calls. For the first couple of months he still carried his phone everywhere he went, as though a journalist would want a quote. He thought it would bother him, this laziness, but it doesn't. He had taken pride in his being a sparky – in being someone who had a real trade, who used his hands – because it set him apart from the smug cunts who sat at a desk for a living; because he had only worn a shirt because he fucking wanted to – Christmas pints at the Rose with the boys – not every day of his life like the rest of them. Of course, none of that matters now. What matters is that he knows how to mend a pipe that has frozen and burst, that he knows how to isolate a short. He spends a couple of hours a day at people's houses, working at these problems with his hands in exchange for a tin of something, or – more often than not – just for a change of conversation. But all this is only to slow the rate of decay, of destruction. The cold is unrelenting.

Rachel used to wake at 6 a.m., every morning, unroll her yoga mat. Arse up in the air. She was always up before him, unless he had to travel to a job. Now she sleeps until he wakes her, like she's waiting for something, and sleeping is just a way of speeding up its arrival. He sits on the edge of the bed and sighs. Trying to provoke her. He can feel her coiled stillness against his lower back.

'Bill is making pancakes,' he says.

She murmurs and turns over, bending herself around him. Her eyes are open, staring blankly into space.

'I hope he stays away. Patrick.'

'He will, if he's got a scrap of fucking sense. I'm going to see Sandra. Mum has declared that she's coming along.'

'Really?' She sits up now, pushing her hair out of her face.

'How am I supposed to stop her?'

'You shouldn't have said anything.'

'I know, I know.'

'I'll come.'

'You want to?'

'It might help. Someone who isn't quite family. Might force her to calm down or something.'

Joe leans in and kisses her. She lies back down, her head in the crook of her arm.

'She's not been herself recently, your mum.'

'What do you mean?' he asks. His voice pitched a little too high, an overextended attempt at nonchalance. He thought that no one else had noticed. And until someone else did it was enough to pretend that he hadn't.

'She just seems a bit vague. And tired all the time.'

Joe takes a breath, but no words present themselves.

'It's probably nothing,' Rachel says.

He breathes out. 'Let's go downstairs, shall we?'

She slides out from behind him and pulls on a dressing gown over her t-shirt and opens the door.

HELEN

She has been thinking about the bears. There have been sightings. None near the village, but people passing through from further north are full of news about them and the mutilated, half-eaten bodies they've left behind. Black eyes against the snow. One bloke talking about them at the Nottage reckoned that the changing winds had confused their sense of direction; he reckoned that the magnetic north pole had shifted and thrown them off kilter. Bill was very indignant and got into a bit of an argument with the man. Said we have enough to worry about without losing our heads over imaginary animal sightings, probably just escaped from the zoo. He started on again about ocean heat sinks and CO_2 absorption levels.

She would like to see one. At a safe distance, of course. She imagines it cresting the roof of the village hall, sliding down the slope – paws splayed – spraying powder and broken tiles in its wake.

The clouds have cleared and the sun is bright now but she can feel the cold through the bottom of the sled. She told Joe that she had hurt her ankle coming down the stairs and wouldn't be able to walk.

Bill had wanted to come with them, but Joe convinced him that it wasn't a good idea. He watched from the window with a teacloth over his shoulder, all the way down the road. He had looked handsome, standing there. His shirt rolled up to his elbows. She likes that he worries about her. Fusses over her. No point in denying it.

She is wearing one of Bill's jumpers and when she buries her chin into her chest she can smell him. An image presents itself: a gull tottering gingerly across the river mud in the grey light of dawn, leaving perfectly formed three-pronged claw prints meandering down towards the water. There must have been a morning, wearing one of his t-shirts.

Joe has the sled rope tied around his waist and Rachel is following behind. She feels like a queen in a litter. As they pass the Nottage she spots the top of the enormous ship's anchor, a fixture on the quayside, poking out of the snow. Almost completely buried now.

One of her first dates with Bill had been crabbing on the quay with the two boys. Ice cream running down over their little wrists. Knobbly knees hanging over the end of the quayside as they cast and recast their lines weighted with mud-caked bacon. Patrick was a little terror, wouldn't sit down for more than a minute before he came running over to pull at Bill's trouser leg, jealous of the attention his dad was paying to her. He had handled the boy with such gentleness, such patience. Joe was muted around Patrick that day. Extra finicky. He wouldn't touch the bacon and, every time he pulled the line up to find some industrious crab had scuttled off with it, he would make her retie it, serious and seemingly pleased that the crab had made its escape. It was around that time, or soon after, when Bill had moved in, that Joe declared he was a vegetarian. The parenting books said it was a way of asserting control, a passing phase. She suspected that he was unhappy about the sudden change in the established rhythms of their shared life, but it was just one of the many ways he questioned things she took for granted. She supposes she was the same with her parents, surprised them in the same way. She hopes she was.

It is so cold, this close to the ground. A wave of nausea passes over her and as it retreats a prickling sensation strobes its way from the tip of her little finger up the side of her right arm, so she grips the sled with her fists. The nausea, and the juddering movement of the sled, makes her grit her teeth and throws her memories into disorder. The vision of the quay dissolves, and in its place the memory of a trip to Southend just after her dad had been diagnosed. New Year's Day and her first hangover from too much schnapps, swallowed in secret trips to the bottom of Sandra's garden; the sickening slow progress of the little train down the length of the pier and the proximity of her mum's pain, which she resented because she didn't know how to respond to it, but which she also envied because of its righteous intensity, which her own feelings couldn't match.

A couple of grockles plod by with their heads bowed in tattered relief-issued snowsuits. She watches them expectantly, but they don't raise their heads in acknowledgement. They won't get on if they don't make an effort.

'Morning,' Joe calls to them. A little too loud, a little too late.

They stop and turn. When they pull down their scarves and pull off their hoods she realises how young they both are, barely eighteen. She mistook their adolescent awkwardness for slouching arrogance. It's so easy to misjudge when everyone is wrapped head to toe the whole time.

'You two off down the Nottage?' Rachel asks. 'The halftracks haven't arrived yet.'

'Nowt to eat,' the older of them says. 'Thought that vicar of yours might have some scraps left.'

'Where you been staying?' Joe says.

The older one nods back in the direction they had come from, up the high street towards the Co-op. 'Found an empty house up that way. Heater had some gas left in it, but it's all gone now. Fucking freezing, come nights. Better than being outside, though. My idiot of a brother here turned his ankle on a railway sleeper. We've been waiting for this next shipment to come in so we can load up on some supplies before we carry on to the exit point.'

'Come up from London way?' Rachel asks.

'Thereabouts. Just east of. We were labouring, Barratt Homes. We thought we would wait it out, until the job started up again.'

'So, this is where optimism landed you,' Joe says, laughing.

The older one smiles, politely. 'We followed the railway tracks. Met some good people along the way. It's further than it looks on the map.'

'Did you see any polar bears?' Helen asks. The young man looks at her, seeming to only now to notice her presence. He looks at Joe – for help, she supposes: who is this old bat and what is she on about? – then back at her.

'We heard someone was killed down on the quay last night,' the younger one pipes up. 'Is it true?'

The older one whacks him in the thigh, trying to shut him up.

'We heard screaming.'

He hits his brother again, a little harder.

She remembers kicking her sister's knees under the bench, that day at the pier, desperately wanting to provoke a reaction, to start a fight so that she could burst into tears and show her mum that she could feel pain too. She needed there to be some fanfare to mark the diagnosis, a boulder thrown into the passing course of their everyday lives so that his death didn't just become a part of that flow – something that might perhaps shake her mum from the sullen, shocked timidity with which she greeted the news so that she might DO SOMETHING, because Helen was still young enough to have a scrap of unexamined faith that her mum could protect her from anything, from time itself. More than anything she needed to punish her mum for keeping her and her sister away from him.

Despite the older brother's shushing of his sibling, his curiosity is evident in his reluctance to move the conversation along.

'There was an accident,' Joe says. Adding, after a moment's pause: 'I think.' He's clearly not ready to own the lie. 'Ask the vicar, I'm sure he'll know more.'

'Alright then,' the older one says. 'We'll let you get on. Nice meeting you all.'

'Nice to meet you,' Rachel says.

'Mind how you go.'

She turns in her sled, craning to watch the two boys pad down the high street. She thinks again that she's about to rob Joe, as well as herself, of the opportunity to say goodbye – the very thing that she held against her own mum for so many years. She is left defenceless without the protection of a diagnosis, the inducement on others to speak in hushed voices and to make a start on the whitewashing process of eulogy, in which all of her petty cruelties, those everyday thoughtless acts, might be embalmed and stowed quietly away. Instead, they'll be thrown into sharper focus by her sudden disappearance, and her betrayal.

'An accident, Joe?' Rachel says.

'Come on, let's keep moving.'

She feels hot even thinking about these things. He is an arm's length away, labouring on her behalf. Up until now she has been glad to ignore her illness. It has allowed her to avoid all the attendant pity. Pity had overtaken her when she had cared for her mum. Despite the obvious fury her mother felt about her condition, Helen couldn't help but let it creep into their interactions – into her own mannerisms, into the way she held her mother – until it came to dictate them.

'Where's Ian's body?' she says.

Joe stops, and turns towards her, his breath clouding the air. 'What?'

She had once read an article in *National Geographic* at the dentist, about Tibetan sky burials, where they just leave the body out in the elements for the birds to eat. Leave it for the birds. She always used to say that to Joe when he dropped food on the floor, so that he wouldn't pick up apple cores covered in dirt from the pavement. Leave it for the birds.

'What are you on about?' he says. Helen gathers she must have spoken aloud without realising it. 'Me and Alfie left it on the side of the river. Put an old dinghy over it.'

'I was just remembering, when you dropped food, how we would say that. Leave it for the birds. It was foxes I was worried about.'

'It will be fine where it is.'

'And what about Sandra? Does she know where he is?'

'No, she doesn't. We're almost there.'

He begins to turn around, but she asks him what he thinks about the polar bears and he stops, the slack of the sled line gathered in his fist. She doesn't want to arrive. She came along because she couldn't see any other way of spending some time with him this morning. She doesn't want to see Sandra. She hadn't considered Alan. Could there be more violence?

'It's a load of old shit. Same as people spotting jaguars and cougars or whatever. Nonsense. Fully grown adults talking this way. Do me a favour.'

He turns back, ploughs on, tension in the set of his jaw.

The cold air catches in her lungs, a tightness that snakes its way from her chest to her throat. She is overtaken by a coughing fit, and Joe stops again and turns to her. She watches his anger dissolve into guilt, as he begins to blame himself for allowing her to come out on this errand into the vicious cold, for his anger which rose up to defy her condition and which disappears in the face of this irrefutable evidence of her decline.

Helen's cheeks are hot. If she can read all this, clear as day, from the weather passing over his features, then:

'How did we miss it, Joe?'

'What?'

'How could we miss what he was going to do?'

'You can hardly blame yourselves,' Rachel says.

'I don't know,' Joe says. 'Here comes Alfie.'

Helen watches his approach, moving slowly through the thick snow. It seems to take an inordinately long time. Alfie starts waving his arms, just for something to do with them,

Helen supposes. His self-conscious false cheer creates a strange festive mood. Waiting at the train station to go to the air show, a knot of excitement.

'We're a bit bloody mob-handed, aren't we?' Alfie says, as he comes to a halt.

'I don't think anyone feels like being stuck indoors – a day like this,' Rachel says.

'I was just talking to Joe about the polar bears,' Helen says.

'Alright there, Helen? How are you?'

'Yes, quite comfortable, thanks, Alfie. How's your mum?'

'Same as ever, same as ever. What was that you said about polar bears?'

'Down at the Nottage. Someone saying they've been spotted further north. Coming down over the ice.'

'Is that right?'

'Enough of this nonsense,' says Joe. 'Let's get moving.'

The morning after Joe's father left for the final time she went to Sandra's house, bringing little Joe along with her. Sandra led him off into the kitchen to make some tea, to give her a moment to herself. She immediately burst into tears, the relief searing her chest, fists clenched to stop herself from crying out. When she looked up Ian was standing in the doorway. Something about his stillness, the steady fascination of his gaze, made her suddenly embarrassed – exposed. She reached into her bag for a tissue, and when she looked up he was gone.

She hopes that she can offer Sandra some comfort. Joe tugs and the sled jolts, the blades coming unstuck from the snow, and they continue their progress up the high street in the bright silence of the morning.

JOE

He knocks once more and leans in. Puts his ear to the door just as it swings open. Alan fills the doorway in his vest. Joe is silenced by the sudden and strange tender whiteness of his skin. The golden tufts of hair on his upper arms.

'What in blessed fuck are you doing here?' Alan says. He studies each of them in turn. Joe has made a mistake in bringing so many people.

'Where is Sandra?' his mother says, as Joe and Alfie help her up from the sled. She totters towards the doorway.

'Didn't bring that cowardly little bastard with you then?'

'Is she upstairs?' Helen moves past Alan into the darkened living room, staring up at the ceiling. Joe moves to follow her but Alan steps back and grabs two fistfuls of his snowsuit, pushing him up against the doorframe.

'What have you done with my boy? Where is he?'

Alan's breath is sour and starchy and his eyes are bloodshot.

'Have you slept?' Joe asks, gently prising Alan's hands from his snowsuit. Alan loses focus and he slopes off into the lounge, falling into an armchair like a sack of flour. Joe hadn't prepared himself for finding Alan in the house. His listless anger makes

Joe feel sick. He realises that he will feel the shock of finding Ian's body again, each time he encounters a new person's grief.

They follow Joe in and squeeze onto the sofa, waiting for him to speak.

'Where is she?' His mum repeats her question but this time directs it at a lampshade. She worries the sleeve of her snowsuit with her fingers. They all face the gas heater, which has taken the place of the TV. A pack of cards fans across the coffee table and onto the floor. Joe feels embarrassed by the warmth of his own body, radiating in the stale air. Rachel catches his eye and looks up towards the ceiling. Joe nods, full of gratitude, and she slips out into the hallway.

'Feels like only last week the two of them were playing silly buggers in the back garden,' Alan says. 'How could this happen?'

'We thought it would be best to have the funeral this afternoon,' Alfie says.

'Today?' Alan asks. 'Who made you Lord of Bloody Everything?'

'Everything is ready,' says Joe. 'It's best we do it straight-away ...' He trails off, unable to find a delicate way to frame their reasoning. 'I'm sorry. The bells will toll when it's time.'

But Alan has turned away, wringing his meaty hands.

'I'll kill him. I'll string that cowardly little toerag up by his ears.'

Alan looks so knackered, folded over his paunch. Joe tries to imagine the fantasies of violence with which he must be sustaining himself. That he is here, sitting on his sofa rather than out in the snow looking for Patrick, reassures him that those fantasies will be as far as it goes. Joe allows himself to wonder, for the first time, whether he would have done the same thing in Patrick's place. If it had been Rachel who had come home with a torn snowsuit, tearful and trembling from cold. He is astonished that it's taken until now to ask himself this directly. When Reg raised it at the Nottage he had pushed the question away as though it were hot. The anger takes its seat in his chest and solidifies into a certainty that he, too, would have killed Ian. Is this why he didn't try to stop Patrick? An instinctual kinship for violence? But when he tries to imagine committing the act itself, the detached part of him takes over and he is watching himself from the outside. The killing is slick: he has simply cast himself in one of the many filmic killings he has watched, sipping beer on the sofa. He feels a surge of sympathy for Alan, trapped in a cycle of impotent imagined revenge.

Rachel appears in the doorway. Alan stares down at his folded hands.

'She's sleeping,' Rachel says.

'I made her take a sleeping pill,' Alan says. 'Found them at the back of the bathroom cupboard.'

'She'll need her strength,' says Helen.

'Even after I brought her back from your place she wouldn't stop,' Alan says. 'Screaming the whole house down. Could hardly bear it.'

'I know, darling, I know.' She leans forward, ever so slowly, and places her small hands on top of his. 'Why don't you tell us about him, Alan? Tell us something you remember about Ian.'

'We never talked much but since the snow we've been' – here he pauses, gulps a lungful of air – 'we had been spending a lot more time together.'

She squeezes his hands once more and Alan begins to tell the story of Joe's seventh birthday party, on the day that

Princess Di died. Joe can recall very little of that day. He can remember waking his mum, watching the news loop over and over with the curtains closed. He remembers that it rained – a thunderstorm – and that they had all rushed in from the garden. But of Ian taking off all his clothes and chasing Naomi around the garden, while Sandra bounded after him, this part of the day has been retold so many times that he can't be sure how much of his memory is a rendering of those retellings.

'I used to tell that story too often. His mother would be after me for winding him up. He always was a little obsessed with that girl,' Alan says, 'we all knew it. He could fixate on things. But he never would have . . .' He falters. 'He couldn't have done what she said.'

Joe believes Naomi. And the strange fact of Alan choosing to tell this story – out of all possible episodes of his son's life which he could have chosen – makes Joe wonder whether Alan might too.

'Are you OK, Helen?' Alan says. He is frowning, and the knuckles of his mum's hands, still resting on Alan's, have turned white. Her head inclines, slowly but steadily, towards Alan's. It seems, for a moment, as though she is going to rest her forehead against his until Joe realises, from the slackness of her jaw, from the discomforting intimacy of this inchoate gesture, that she is about to fall from the arm of the chair.

He jumps up and catches her around the shoulders, drawing her backwards and up onto her feet. She bats him away, tottering over to the sofa and lowering herself down into the place he has left.

All of this Alan watches with a look of distaste; the frustration

45

of a child who has lost the attention of those around them. He gets to his feet and lurches off towards the kitchen.

'We'll have a fucking drink then, shall we?' Alan says. 'A toast to my boy.'

Joe looks at his mum. She is nodding off. When was the last time she left the house? Amid the wreckage of this living room, her frailty is all too obvious. He feels Rachel's gaze on him and as he catches her eye, she gives him a look – half-grimace, half-smile – you might give when you accidentally make eye contact with someone on the bus.

'Sherry'll do you?' Alan says. 'We've got a little left. Sandra's ma liked it at Christmas.'

He lays five glasses out on the coffee table, sending yellowing copies of the *Daily Mail* and *TV Choice* cascading to the floor. Joe casts around for something to say; a high-vis coat hangs from the back of the door.

'When did they close the quarry?' Joe asks.

'Close? When did they stop paying us, you mean? Must have been about two months after the snow started. Most people had stopped coming into work by then anyway. Packing up getting ready to go to wherever-the-fuck. No fuel for the diggers. We shouldn't have stayed.'

'We used to go and play down there,' Joe says. 'We'd see Ian sometimes.'

Alan grunts as he sucks his drink down, a slight sob escaping him as he slams the empty glass onto the table, picking up the one he had placed in front of Helen.

'What gives you the right to talk about him? After what your brother did?' He pauses, and takes another gulp, continuing in a smaller voice. 'I was too soft with him.'

'Don't start down that road,' says Helen.

'I'm going to check on Sandra again, see if she is awake,' says Rachel.

'Have you heard about the bears, Alan?' Helen says.

'Bears?'

'Mum, I don't think this is the time.'

'What do you mean, bears?'

'Sandra told me you'd been down to London awhile. I wondered if you had heard anything about the polar bears coming over from Norway.'

Alan has stopped listening and has begun muttering to himself once more. Joe looks over at his mum but she shrugs her shoulders as if to say 'I tried'. She has never really liked him, Joe realises now. One of those things that you're blind to in your parents, the revelation of which arrives with a feeling of loss.

'Bugger this,' Helen says, and struggles to her feet, following Rachel from the room.

HELEN

Sandra is buried under a mound of duvets and quilts and Rachel is at the window, looking out over the street. Helen leans in the doorway, catching her breath.

'Still sleeping?' she says.

Rachel jumps, her arms coming up to protect her chest, her stomach. She laughs.

Helen joins Rachel by the radiator. It feels to her as though it takes an eternity, as though Rachel is watching her down the length of a tunnel. But then suddenly she is beside her, and the radiator is cold beneath her fingertips. The view is a shoddy reproduction of the street. The snow creating white approximations of the houses, cars and walls that it blankets.

'Don't worry, he puts me on edge too,' she whispers.

'It's everything. Everything has got me tense today,' Rachel says. They stand in silence, side by side, their breath fogging the glass. 'It was awkward, with those grockles earlier.'

'It's hard to know what to say. I'm still trying to get my head around it.'

'Joe didn't need to lie.'

'They were just being nosy; it's none of their business.

I think Joe was right not to get into it. We don't need more trouble.'

'I envied them.' Rachel pauses. 'Just a little bit. They'll have moved on in a couple of days. This will be forgotten.'

'Do you ever wish that you had left? Right at the beginning?'

Helen can feel Rachel studying her face, perhaps to see if she's joking. They don't have this kind of relationship – the kind where you can ask such candid questions.

'We talked about it. I don't know whether Joe would have ever mentioned this, but yeh, we discussed it. He wanted to wait and see what happened. Didn't want to panic. So, we waited, and then the decision was made for us.'

Her arms are crossed over her chest and Helen realises that Rachel has taken her question as a veiled plea: don't leave us. She feels the guilt rise again and tries to figure out how to put the conversation onto a different track.

'Have you heard anything recently from your mum?'

'Most days, when the phone masts are up.'

'They must be in Spain by now? How is it?'

'Warmer,' she laughs. 'Things are OK, I think. They're still being moved around a lot, which is difficult for my dad.'

Across the street, a fox appears in the aperture of a broken window. It pads across the roof of a car buried by the snow and turns down the street, following the line of houses with a jauntiness that makes Helen smile. She marvels at the ease with which it moves through its new surroundings, as though nothing has changed at all. She doesn't believe in God, but there is something in the animal's grace – the russet flash of its tail as it disappears around the corner seems brushed with perfection.

The trail of paw prints is erased by fresh snow. It has started

49

again, a brief flurry. Its constant movement transfixes her. She finds herself standing at the window of their bedroom, tracing and retracing the old course of the river, losing and finding it again, until her edges blur and the minutes flatten out into hours. Mornings pass this way.

'I tried to sell makeup to the lady who lived in that house once,' Helen says. 'When I was doing Avon. She was a right bitch.' She takes a deep breath. 'Rachel, I'm sorry that I haven't asked more often, about your parents.'

'Did my mum ever buy anything from you?'

The question surprises Helen. 'I'm not sure I ever tried to sell to her. We were never that close, not back then. Your parents had their friends from the university. And it was hardest selling to acquaintances, harder than friends or strangers. Because you'd know you'd see them again, and the first thing that would pop into their heads would be "here comes the bloody Avon lady".'

'Well, Mum has missed her chance forever, I guess,' Rachel laughs. 'I don't see Avon coming out the other side of this.'

Helen sits on the end of the bed and lays a hand on Sandra's leg, feeling the faint warmth through the blankets.

'All I was trying to say is, I know it must be difficult. Being apart from them.'

'It is. I miss them. And I feel guilty, being apart from them.' Rachel pauses. 'What's going to happen, do you think?'

The moment has arrived to announce: I'm leaving. She repeats it to herself as she had in her bedroom, and it retains the air of a protective charm. She turns to look at Sandra to make sure that she's still sleeping.

'Had Naomi mentioned anything before, about Ian acting inappropriately?'

Rachel snorts – perhaps at the question, perhaps at its obvious evasion. Helen is never sure when she has let too much time pass before giving an answer anymore. Rachel drops her voice to a whisper.

'He always had a thing for Naomi,' Rachel says. 'Ever since we were kids. But I never thought he could be capable of trying to force things with her.'

'The number of conversations Sandra and I had about it when you were children. About trying to bring him out of his shell.'

'But Patrick,' Rachel says, 'I never could have imagined . . . such *violence*. What happened? When did he become a person who could do something like that?'

'Growing up with people, you're so close that it's impossible to pinpoint the moment they changed. And then they do something and you wring your hands trying to find signs . . . Darling, I don't know.'

Sandra groans and turns over and they both look back to see if she'll wake, but in a moment she is snoring softly once more. Helen knows that they should wake her, but the longer they sit here together the more difficult it seems.

'When she got together with Alan, we were only eighteen. I didn't like him, and I told her as much. We fell out over it. And here we are thirty-five years later. They're still together. And that's something that has been between us all this time.'

Rachel laughs, grim, and says: 'I guess you never know which out of the hundreds of things that come out of your mouth each day will stick.'

She takes a breath, as though she's about to say something else, but then laughs again instead, shaking her head. Helen places a hand on her shoulder and gives her a little squeeze.

'Thanks for coming to stay with us, for not pressuring Joe to leave with your parents. I'm sure that you could have convinced him, if you had chosen to.'

Rachel starts to protest but Helen interrupts.

'I know it can't have been easy. Moving back into his childhood bedroom. All of his old things. Putting up with me and Bill.'

Rachel puts a hand over Helen's. The moment is passing. But the openness that she has had to adopt to bring herself to the point of telling Rachel has lent them an intimacy that she can't bear to disrupt. She wishes that she had tried to get closer to Rachel before today. Even as she thinks this there is a stab of maternal jealousy. What has she said to Joe that will count, in the end?

Sandra yawns and shifts again. A small, wounded cry follows. It's a sound so desolate that Rachel and Helen turn slightly away from one another, embarrassed, almost, to have heard it. She has woken, then. And remembered.

'Let me deal with her,' Helen whispers. 'Why don't you go and see how the others are getting on?'

When Rachel has left her side she takes a couple of deep breaths, then climbs onto the bed next to Sandra, lying down on top of the covers. The crenelated ceiling has the same effect as the snow, of displacement. She wonders how much of their conversation Sandra heard. It can't hurt, Helen thinks. To hear these things, but indirectly; to be able to face them only so far as your strength will allow.

She turns onto her side, puts her arms around Sandra and feels her body tense against her touch. They lie this way, silent and still, until Sandra relents and relaxes into Helen's arms, making that same keening sound from the back of her throat.

Stroking her hair, Helen realises that she hasn't been so close to Sandra in a long time. The smell of Sandra, her perfume (did she remember to apply some, even in the midst of all this? Or is Helen's imagination supplying the rose and patchouli it expects to find under the musk of just-woken sourness?), makes her think of the time she held Sandra's hair back in the toilets at the Greyhound when she threw her guts up, sobbing, laughing, on her eighteenth birthday; of standing behind Sandra at her dressing table – still in place in the corner of the bedroom – on the morning of her wedding day, drinking cava as she painted her nails; of waking, next to her, on New Year's Day, with the taste of peach schnapps and her thundering blood in the back of her throat. This will be the last time she combs Sandra's hair with her fingers.

Pain falls like shadow, but the warmth and familiarity of Sandra's body is lulling her to sleep. She resists, then relents.

JOE

Alan has fallen asleep in the armchair. Pissed and knackered. Together he and Alfie had tried to draw him onto other topics, onto the scavenging trips that he had taken with Ian along the tracks to London, scouring the huge warehouses ringing the city; onto other, more distant memories of the pits; onto, at last, the snow itself. But Joe knows so little about Alan beyond the scraps of gossip he overheard as a child. He had never paid attention to him. By the time Alan had finished his glass of sherry he was back to muttering veiled threats into his chest. Joe takes a swig from the bottle of sherry and passes it to Alfie.

'Should we go outside?' Alfie says. 'Looks like he'll be out for a while.'

Joe nods at the gas burner. 'You really want to leave this, to go out there?'

Alfie laughs. 'Just figured we should go and find out what people are going to say, when the halftracks arrive.'

Joe feels caught out, as though he has put his comfort before Patrick's safety. He points up at the ceiling. 'I'm her ride home.'

Alfie scoops the cards off the card table and starts to collect the ones on the floor. 'May as well get comfortable then.'

'On the way here we ran into two grockles. Young lads, brothers. They asked about what had happened yesterday. And without thinking about it I lied.'

Alfie deals. 'What do you mean?'

'I said there was an accident. Told them to ask the vicar.'

'There was a lot of noise. I did wonder who else might have heard.'

'I feel bad for implicating the vicar.'

'He'll know what to say.'

Joe throws the cards down. 'Sorry, mate, I'm so fucking sick of playing cards.'

'Yeh, me too. I'm starting to miss things that I thought were totally shit. Like daytime TV. To be sat with a cup of tea in front of a rerun of *Homes Under the Hammer* right now.' Alfie sucks in his cheeks.

'Those lads said they heard screaming. Where were you when you first heard the noise?'

'Honestly, I thought it was foxes fucking, the sound that Ian was making. I was just sat with my mum, in the kitchen. And then Patrick was shouting. By the time I got my snowshoes on all I could see was Patrick's back, that fuck-off great axe swinging beside him.'

'I didn't hear anything until they were out on the river ice. The noise of the generator is too loud at my house.'

'It'll be one of those "do you remember where you were when" moments,' Alfie says. 'Like, do you remember the night that Obama was elected?'

'Really? We're gonna talk about Obama now?' Joe says.

'Yeh, first time, 2008. Who remembers the second time? I bought a ten bag and we stayed up.'

'I remember. It was Guy Fawkes. People were setting off fireworks across the river, when we were out in front of the house smoking.'

'Next day in college everyone was fucking jubilant. Like he had just cured cancer or something.'

'What do you remember about the day that Diana died?' Joe says. 'The day that I had the birthday party Alan was talking about?'

'I don't really remember the party itself. I do remember the morning, seeing it on the news. Being pissed off that there were no cartoons on so going to wake up my mum. I thought it was weird that everyone was so upset about it, I didn't really understand who she was.'

Rachel pokes her head around the door.

'How's she doing?' Joe asks.

'Your mum is going to stay with her for a while, I think.'

She squeezes onto the sofa between him and Alfie. Alfie offers her the bottle. She wrinkles her nose.

'A little early in the day for me.'

Alfie laughs and Joe takes the bottle from him. Joe puts a hand on Rachel's knee and she nestles into his shoulder.

'We were doing "where you were when",' Alfie says.

'9-11 is the big one,' Rachel says.

'First week of secondary school,' Joe says. 'Went round to Ryan's house – you remember Ryan? – for some squash and snacks or whatever and arrived just as the second plane hit. At least that's how I remember it. His mum had it on the TV in the kitchen with the sound down.'

'Yeh, I found out when I got home,' says Alfie. 'Mum sitting in front of the TV with a glass of wine.'

'Ryan's mum used to paint birds on pieces of driftwood and they were all over the house,' Joe says. 'I wonder where she is now.'

He also remembers that when he got home his dad had been there, standing by the sink. And that he had stayed the night, but was gone again in the morning. And that Mum had kept sighing and muttering about how terrible it was that so many people had been lost, watching the planes smash into the towers over and over again as they ate their cereal. He had felt alienated from her sadness and guilty that he couldn't feel anything for the people who had died, not understanding the overlap of her own private sadness, and repressing his own.

But instead of saying any of this he squeezes Rachel's knee and asks: 'What about you?'

'I was in Florida, on holiday.'

'Disneyworld?'

'Yeh. Furious because I was missing the start of school. Everyone went mad. Buying everything in the supermarket. Do you remember where you were the day it first started snowing?'

'I was driving back from a job,' Joe says. 'I remember seeing that the daffodils had just come up – on the roundabout by Tesco – and then all I was worried about was that ours wouldn't survive the freeze.'

'I honestly can't remember,' Alfie says. 'Didn't really seem like an event, in itself, at the time. It's not like it had never snowed before. Like, I remember a few bits and pieces from right at the start. Going sledding. That lock-in at the Rose when we drank the bar dry, last of the beer. First time the power went out. Yeh. And when the power went out for good. Who doesn't remember shit like that . . .' He trails off for a moment. 'Those nights that they had at the bookshop, under camping lights we charged up at the Nottage, with the pantomime group from the William Loveless hall. It was like a holiday, at that point. I felt frantic and manic all the time. Like a holiday that had run out of control.'

They are silent for a moment, listening to the sound of Alan's steady breath.

'How about the day they announced they were suspending parliament?' Joe says.

'We watched the PM's announcement together, Joe,' says Rachel. 'On TV. Still had TV then. That happened pretty early on. That's one thing I'm glad of, that I'm no longer constantly presented with that man's smug, complacent face as he walks us over the edge of the cliff.'

'Do you think we'll have this same conversation,' Alfie says, 'in fifteen years' time? Like: as far as we understood, it wasn't supposed to start snowing and just not stop. And laugh, at how fucking naïve we were. Like children. Crying at the TV.'

Alfie takes the bottle back from Joe and has a swig. Joe feels Rachel shrink against him, only very slightly, and is suddenly aware of the low, warm buzz from the sherry and a feeling of him and Alfie being slightly out of step with her, and with the tone of the occasion.

'Have you heard about what happened on Jersey?' Rachel says.

'I stopped reading the news when all of it was about us, and all of it was bad,' Joe says.

'There was an outbreak of flu, and they quarantined the island.'

'Holding people there?' Alfie says.

'That's what I read. No one is allowed on or off. Downloaded the news on my phone yesterday, at the Nottage.'

Rachel takes her phone from inside her snowsuit and finds the piece for Alfie to read, handing it to him.

'Well, fuck.'

Joe is surprised that she has thought to bring her phone. He has stopped reading the news as well. Events seem frictionless. On a clear day, when the masts are up, if you've remembered to charge your phone at the Nottage, you can still follow what is happening. But he has lost any sense of investment in anything that happens outside the village, and even feels a sense of resentment whenever he sees Rachel on her phone. He has stopped asking her about her parents. He feels it coming between them, this turning away, but he can't seem to turn himself back. When travellers arrive along the tracks, headed to the coast, and people gather down at the Nottage to share news and rumours, he finds reasons to excuse himself, clearing the fresh snowfall or checking inventory.

She was always more social, more engaged. She used to call him Captain Ostrich. He hasn't heard that one in a while. At the beginning, before the government moved to the Continent, when there was still electricity at home, they would tune in to watch the Prime Minister's briefing every day. They would laugh at his bluster; the way his address to camera imitated a leader in a post-apocalyptic blockbuster. Joe doesn't know exactly when these briefings stopped, as he had ceased tuning in when it became clear that life wasn't going back to normal any time soon. If ever.

One year. That's all that has passed, to come to this.

There's a light knock at the window; everyone flinches and looks over at Alan, but he continues to snore away. Bill's face appears at the frosted glass, his hand shielding his eyes against the glare.

HELEN

She wakes from a dream of flying to find that Sandra is no longer asleep, but is propped up against the pillows, staring straight ahead.

'Sandra?' Helen says, as gently as she can. Sandra looks down at her, following the sound of her voice.

'What are you doing here?' she asks. Her face is expressionless, her voice flat.

'I came to see if you were OK,' Helen begins – Sandra's eerie, shellshocked stillness has thrown her. She is always at her most vague when she has just woken. Wailing and crying is one thing, but this she doesn't know how to help with. 'To see if I could do anything.'

'You came to see if I was OK.' Sandra repeats her words back at her; her even tone mocks their inadequacy.

Helen is suddenly embarrassed to have fallen asleep next to her. What kind of message does that send? She is embarrassed to have thought that she could offer Sandra any comfort. It's clear to her, now, she came for the benefit of her own conscience. But she can't think of anything to say – what is there that she possibly can say? – can't think of anything, in fact, other than that she needs to get out of there.

'OK, well, if there's nothing else.' Helen pauses, to give Sandra a chance to soften, to open up – but she gives nothing. The awkwardness is painful. 'I'll see you later.' She shuffles towards the door, turning for one last look at her friend, whose gaze is fixed on the middle distance. She thought she would have more time.

In the living room she finds Alan, alone, fast asleep in the arm-chair. The heater has been put out and someone has laid a duvet over him. They've all gone – a sense of rising panic. Have they left her? She starts to try to calculate whether she could make it home under her own power. It has been . . . she has no idea when she last walked that far. She shivers as she crosses the room to the window, stepping carefully to avoid Alan's outstretched legs.

Bill. Just across the street, thank god. She slips out the front door like a thief in the night.

'Joe went on ahead, with Rachel,' he stage-whispers. 'He wanted to wait for you, but I told him to go on. He said I should wait for you to come out, that I was an idiot to come here. That Alan would see me and think of Patrick, and it would set him off again. He's right, of course, but I was going mad just wait-ing around at home. I couldn't help myself.' He seems frantic, distracted. 'I was going to wait around the corner for you all to come out but then I saw Joe through the window and I just thought . . . Is he still asleep? Did you speak to Sandra?'

'I thought everyone had left me.' Helen hears her voice wobble. She is furious at herself for this self-pity, for her obvious vulnerability.

'Oh, I'm sorry, my love. I should have told Joe to let you know I was outside.' Bill takes her hands and pulls her in, hugging her to his chest. 'Come on, let's get out of here.'

As Bill lowers her to the sled, the image of Alan asleep in the armchair, his head lolling to the side and his mouth hanging open, stays with her. What might have happened had she allowed things to go further, that night he had kissed her? There had been a moment where her curiosity as to what Sandra found exciting about Alan had lost the battle against her mounting disgust and she pulled away. He has never forgiven her for that rejection. Helen suspects that, on some level, Sandra has always known what is behind his gruffness towards her, the way that he will always find an excuse to leave any room that she enters at the earliest possible moment – and so Helen has, in her turn, always resented Alan for the distance his anger opened up between her and Sandra. She thinks of other men in her life who she has rejected and can't think of any who responded other than with astonished anger.

If they had raised a child together, would he resemble Ian? Would he have carried himself with the same stealthiness? She has never heard Alan shout but she has no trouble imagining one hundred scenarios in which he would raise his voice.

There is another possibility, of course: that had things gone further with Alan she might have left the village entirely. She might have bought a motorbike, moved to London. She might never have met David, never had Joe. Perhaps Sandra would have broken it off with Alan and Ian would never have been born. Perhaps this winter would have passed, like every other before it, into another spring while she continued on in uninterrupted clear health, in unbroken lucidity, living her alternate life away from the cold which bites now at the tender skin of her lips and her eyelids, away from the pain which makes time lurch like an injured animal, coming home at the end of the day to gather clean linen off the line and press them to her face to inhale its windblown freshness. She could be an actress, or perhaps a civil servant. Or she could even be a painter. After all, this alternate self would never have met David, never been exposed to his agonised abstractions, his bitter disappointments and self-loathing; she might be able to imagine for herself an art which didn't consist of brash colours and clumsy contours. Something that might capture the delicacy of the river, or the quiet dunnish beauty of the marsh now smothered by the ice and the snow.

Helen looks about her. On one side of the road the snowdrifts run all the way up to the eaves of the houses and it is only the slope of the roofs and the indignant chimneystacks pointing skyward like accusing fingers that give any suggestion that there were ever any houses there at all. She doesn't recognise any of it. She doesn't know where she is.

'Where is Joe? Where is Rachel?'

'They went ahead, down to the pyre. Check everything is ready for the funeral.'

She feels panicked. What did their visit achieve? She fell asleep beside Sandra. Joe had a drink with Alan. What does any of it amount to?

'Where are we going?' she says. 'Why are we going towards the top of the village?'

Bill stops for a second and turns to look down at her, in the sled.

'What are you on about? That's the other direction. We're headed towards the quay.'

'Oh right, yes of course. I must have dozed off.'

'We're going to see Patrick and Naomi. Over at Bowyer's farm.'

Bill offers a smile that doesn't quite reach his eyes. They could be right around the corner from the house and she would have no idea. Nothing looks the same. The snow has reshaped the streets which she has walked every day of her life, which she has been walking from her bed since the pain first started, going over and over every word said in anger or in love to try to find the event that set everything in motion. At least, that has been the excuse she rehearses every time her name spoken by Bill or by Joe recalls her to a room that she had vacated unaware. Off looking for clues. She can't remember the last time she left the house. It might have been two months ago or six.

This erasure of the village is a mirror sickness of her own; the place has been stripped of the details that order her memories of her life here.

She wishes she could be at work right now, in the break room, laughing at a GIF of a baby otter or a basket of sleepy puppies. When they first started seeing each other Bill would send these kinds of things to her. She would sit with a Kit-Kat emailing back and forth. They would create characters who would last a couple of weeks and then fall into the background, supporting players in the story of their growing intimacy. One of the qualities she had immediately liked about him was that he quite clearly didn't have a need to be taken seriously. He was the polar opposite of David. And his work was just something he did. It didn't have to be enshrined as some sort of proof of the validity and worth of his existence. The thought of David sending her a picture of dozy owls is hard to conceive. He might spend three weeks painting a floor-to-ceiling abstract on the agony of his love for her, but he wouldn't have been able to see the simple charm of a baby animal.

Bill went off in the morning and came back in the evening and that was the end of it. They would watch TV or talk about the news or about the boys or about where they might go on holiday. Daydreaming about buying things they could never afford: a caravan or a boat.

She misses that time away from each other. It gave grain to their existence. The smooth manner in which the days glide between them now provides no opportunity for renewal.

She thinks of how many Saturday mornings Bill spent washing his car, of how each time there was heavy rainfall she would be running calculations before she could stop herself to try and figure out whether she could afford the repairs if the gutters were finally to break, of the afternoon she spent crying down the phone to the gas company when they overestimated her bill, six months after David had finally left for good.

Naomi will be there, with Patrick. She hasn't considered that till now. Helen wonders what she might possibly say to her. She knows her so little as an adult. And she was a quiet child. Her parents left months ago so she'll have no one to talk to about what has happened other than Patrick and – though she feels a sense of responsibility – Helen is not sure she has the energy to comfort or reassure her. She doesn't know how to play this role, as mother to women.

Naomi's dad Robert worked at the university. He always said very little and drank too much whenever they were at parties for the children. His fist clamped around a wine glass, a fixed, red-faced expression of private amusement. She never liked him, without knowing why. The resentment bubbles back up. Perhaps this is why she has held herself at a distance from Naomi.

'Look,' Bill says.

They have stopped at the top of the narrow lane that leads down to the quayside. She sees the white plume of the buried fig tree to the left, where it once leaned over the wall dropping its fruit onto the cracked tarmac in the summer. Passing cars would crush them and release their perfume. At the bottom the sign for the pub hangs only a couple of feet from the ground. She wants the smell of hot vinegar and paper and river-licked mud, to taste the first acrid sip of a can of Diet Coke. There is a sudden pain in her chest. A weight. In these moments she can't tell if the pain is the illness or a knot of something else. Bill climbs into the sled behind her, scooting her bum forward.

'What are you doing?' she asks.

Without a word Helen feels the sled tip forward and she leans back into Bill as her stomach climbs upward to displace the weight in her chest and she is laughing; as they careen down the hill she squints her eyes against the glare of the ash-grey clouds. Bill's boots drop from the rails of the sled to the snow, kicking powder up into her hair and her mouth and turning them ninety degrees to come to a skidding stop at the bottom of the hill in front of the pub.

She can feel Bill's chest rise and fall. She would like to stay like this and let the snow bury them, to take them as it has Bill's car, their unpaid bills, all their precious guttering, and make them a blip on this new landscape, a landmark for whoever will bear the responsibility of inheriting it.

Bill shuffles to his feet and she sits up. A small crowd has formed in front of the Nottage, people milling about. She searches but cannot see any sign of Joe or Rachel.

'Word must be getting around, about the funeral,' Bill says.

'Not much else for people to be doing, I suppose, aside from standing at their windows and staring at the horizon. Waiting for something to happen.'

'Come on, we best be getting on. Before anyone sees us.'

Bill picks up the rope and turns the sled, taking them in the opposite direction along the quay towards the marshes, and the farm beyond.

JOE

'Can we go through the playing fields? Might make a nice change,' Rachel says.

'It will be quicker to go straight down the high street,' Joe says. 'Come on. I'm cold. I want to get home.'

'Joe, wait.'

'What?' He can feel the frustration in his shoulders and the doubling of it from making Rachel bear the brunt of it.

'Can we just take a breather? For five minutes?'

He turns back and sighs, pulling up his snood against the wind.

'Five minutes,' she continues. 'What difference is five minutes going to make?'

Joe softens. 'Spun out?'

'Spun and done.'

She's right, of course. Joe knows that his first instinct since yesterday has been to propel himself at the highest possible speed from event to event in order to avoid thinking about the choices he is making; to avoid, in fact, admitting to himself that he is making any choices at all.

The tops of the football goalposts are still visible. Rachel makes for one of them. She clears some snow with her glove and sits on the crossbar, the fabric of her snowsuit making a crackling sound, sticking and ripping from the frozen metal as she settles herself.

The contours of the accumulated snow have preserved the slight slope of the playing fields running down towards the train tracks. Off to the right the woods are denuded. They look like the pictures from those First World War battlefields where the trees have been utterly blown to shit. This is the result of inexpert woodcutters desperate for fuel, wielding blunt axes with cold, unresponsive fingers. There is something indecent about the flesh of the naked trees, stripped of their bark, like injured fingers rising above the crust of snow.

He looks for the pebbledash slabs that, mysteriously, had been stacked in haphazard fashion at the treeline. Completely buried now. They had made a perfect den for eating penny sweets and setting small fires with stolen cigarette lighters. Alfie had once told him that they were demolished gravestones after they had watched a rental copy of *From Dusk Till Dawn* that his dad had left lying around the house. It was the first time Joe had ever seen a dildo. After the film had ended Alfie ran upstairs and came back wielding one that they marvelled over together for five minutes until they were interrupted by the doorbell. They never talked about it again.

'It's strange how calm your mum is about all of this. Sandra is her best friend. She's known Ian since he was born.'

Joe sits down next to her, to make it easier to avoid her gaze.

Rachel continues: 'I think she's getting worse.'

'I don't think any of us know how to behave,' he says. There is a certain strain in his mother's relationship with Sandra: one of those passive-aggressive competitive friendships, where every comment ends with an epithet that sounds like a veiled threat. Darling. Hun.

'I just find it strange is all,' Rachel says.

'What can any of us do, at this point?'

'If there is anything that we can take from the past two days surely it's that ignoring a problem won't make it disappear.'

Joe once threw a locked briefcase full of partially burnt porn from the old shipyard wharf into the river. The memory of this moment – of the harrowing self-consciousness he felt carrying the case down the quay after dark, of the slickness of the plastic handle in his sweaty palm, of watching the briefcase spin and tumble through the air before splashing into the river, where it bobbed, lazily in the current – feathers its way down his throat. He pulls his hand from his mitten to tug on his nose to choke off the tickle of hysterical laughter.

'Did I ever tell you about . . .' Joe begins, but pulls up when he catches Rachel's eye and is reminded of the truancy of his thoughts. He had found the scraps of porn in one of the old shipyard sheds, left by older kids who would steal packs of fags and magazines from the sweetshop when the owner went into the backroom. He stuffed them in his pockets and brought them home, hiding them in a briefcase – next to some short stories he had written, some stones he had found on a trip to the beach – which he had bought in a charity shop. In his den under his bed, he would take out the scraps and try to make sense of the tangled limbs, ringed and pocked with burn marks, feeling both excitement and disgust. Eventually, he lost interest. The briefcase was forgotten until it was unearthed when he had outgrown the bed and he was clearing the space underneath ready for the arrival of a new one. He had forgotten the combination.

And it was in this panic, in this spirit of stale excitement and disgust, that he made his trip to the old wharf and cast the briefcase into the river.

He realises that Rachel is still staring at him, expectantly. He works his jaw with his numb fingers, as though he is trying to mechanically dislodge the smile that is frozen there.

'Are you OK?' she says. 'Did you ever tell me about what?'

'It doesn't matter. Sorry. I got distracted.'

'See. This is what I mean. Every time I bring it up you deflect. You try to turn away.'

'Well, what difference would it make if we were able to get some kind of diagnosis? What purpose would that serve other than to make her and all the rest of us miserable when we have to confront the fact that there are no drugs? No hospital to go to.'

'Joe.'

'Where would we even take her to get a diagnosis?' he says. 'The halftracks only come in once a fortnight. Maybe there will be a doctor with them today, maybe not. There hasn't been for months.'

'Joe, I need to tell you something.'

'Now that I think about it, Alfie was saying that old Dr Watts might still be kicking about, that she hadn't followed the evacuation order.'

'Joe!'

He turns to her and takes her hands. He can see that she is close to tears. He feels a familiar onrush of guilt. He scans his memory of the last few days to try to pinpoint a moment where he had been particularly inconsiderate but draws a blank. This, he knows, is damning in itself. His face screws itself into an expression somewhere between a smile and a grimace.

She takes a deep breath: 'I think I'm pregnant.'

'What?' Joe laughs, knowing immediately that this is the wrong response. 'Sorry, I mean are you sure?' He winces, wrong again. The fact is that a wave of ecstasy is passing up through his stomach to his throat and he doesn't know what to do about it. He can feel it spilling down the length of his arms into his fingertips, which are gripping Rachel's hands too hard. He's aware that he should say something else but now he finds he can't say anything at all and he's laughing again and shaking and the tears that were welling in Rachel's eyes are now spilling down her cheeks, freezing in her eyelashes.

'You're crying,' she says.

'No, *you're* crying.'

'I don't know for sure yet,' she says. 'I don't have a test. But my period was due weeks ago. It's so weird, not being able to test it. Used to be able to track every slight shift in temperature, now I can't even get a stick to pee on.'

'Have you told your mum yet?'

Rachel takes her phone from her pocket and clicks the screen on, and then off again. 'No, not yet. I wanted to tell you first. I didn't want to tell you today, but I couldn't wait any longer. I don't have anyone to talk to, apart from you.'

She sobs, and then laughs. Joe puts his arms around her. That wave breaks again, making him press his knees together as he squeezes her through her snowsuit. He doesn't quite feel it's safe to say anything else just yet.

'I think it would break my mum's heart,' she says, 'is the other thing. To know that she won't be here. Never missed her more than now. Never felt more guilty that I'm not with her.'

'I know, my love, I know.'

She looks up at him.

'This is a good thing, isn't it?' she says.

'It's a good thing.'

'My toes are getting cold.'

'We should get moving, then.'

'I'll stop off at the Nottage and call my mum. Would rather not do it at the house with everyone breathing down my neck. Your mum actually asked me earlier whether I had spoken to her recently. Doesn't feel real, it won't until I tell her.' She rubs at her thighs. 'And it's at least warm at the Nottage.'

'I can handle the preparations for the funeral, get everything ready. Move the . . .' He falters. 'Move Ian.'

For a moment, neither of them gets up. A moment of quiescence while the terrible events of the past couple of days are held in balance by this new revelation. Then Joe stands, looking down at Rachel. As she scans the maimed treeline a snowflake catches on her eyelashes. The sun, now almost directly above, picks out each detail of the delicate frozen latticework. She smiles, holds out her hand and Joe lifts her to her feet from the goalpost.

HELEN

Helen had never really liked Nicky Bowyer, but she had assumed that Nicky would always be one of those people in her outer orbit. The kind you can never quite free yourself of because of birthday parties or funerals or craft fairs or those other village occasions which throw you in with people who you still resent for obscure reasons, like they used to dot their i's with hearts or their child once made yours cry at nursery school. They had some money – Nicky always seemed to be driving a new car – so Helen shouldn't have been surprised when she left, but it still felt like a betrayal. Nicky was definitely one of the first to start voting Tory. She can picture her with a rosette standing outside the village hall.

It is almost silent, as they reach Bowyer's farm. This far from the village the metronome of the generator has blurred to a distant hum. They have followed the river course away from the quayside, past the new houses and down towards the creek. Before they turned inland to cross the marsh, Bill pulled the sled around and they looked back at the village. It occurred to Helen that this is the farthest that she has been from the house in almost a year.

The tops of the hawthorns that lined the lane running from the main road to the farm are still visible, two lines of stunted battlements in the snow. A series of increasingly hysterical hand-painted signs nailed to trees leading up to the house, warning outsiders about the dogs and the shotguns. She was right, she thinks, about Nicky; she *would* put up signs.

The farm looks entirely desolate. The snow has climbed to the first floor. Aside from the column of black smoke rising from the chimney stack, curling back in the direction of the village, there is no indication that anyone is inside.

Bill points up at the smoke. 'They'll be able to see that from the quay.'

'People'll just think it's grockles. And anyway, who's looking for them?'

'Come on, let's get inside.'

When Bill helps her to her feet, she discovers that they have gone completely numb. The cold has got into her bones, she has been still too long. It's so dangerous, how quickly it can happen. There were some close calls in the first few months: folk getting lost on their way home from the Nottage after a few drinks. Or people who simply stopped in the snow for a rest, not recognising the signs, the creeping drowsiness. She feels a little confused.

Off to their right, a window swings open. Patrick's face appears.

'You might have called out,' he says. 'I had no idea who was coming.'

He leans further out, scanning the lane behind them.

'No one else with us, son.'

Patrick hops out of the window. In his hand is the axe.

Bill's eyes are fixed on it; he is shaking his head, a look of thunder on his face. 'Patrick, what are you still doing with that thing?'

'As I said. Didn't know who was coming.'

Bill holds out his hand. 'Proud of what you done, are you? Holding onto that like some kind of sick memento?' Patrick straightens up – instinctual pride – but then relents, holding the axe out to his dad, handle first. As Bill takes it, Patrick's shoulders sag, the weight of it gone. He looks somehow both older and younger.

Without another word, Bill walks around the side of the house. Helen tries to figure out what it might mean, that Patrick has held onto the axe. He steps out of the shadow cast by the farmhouse, hands on his hips: restless.

He has washed his face and is wearing a clean snowsuit – must have taken it from the house – but his neck still glimmers with dried blood, his hair slick in places. It's become so much more difficult to keep clean.

Bill reappears; he offers his empty hands. 'Last we'll see of that thing.'

'I know it must seem a little mad. It's just, after I . . . I didn't want Naomi to have to suffer more for what I done. If anyone had come after me.'

'So she's safer with that bloody great axe in the house, is she? Planned to take on the whole village?'

'How will we cut firewood?'

Helen catches Bill's eye. He sighs and throws up his hands. She doesn't want him to lose his temper with Patrick, not now; he would only regret it later. It's clear that there is only so much punishment that the boy can take at this point. Now that the

76

axe has been removed, Patrick seems to have collapsed in on himself entirely.

'Can we come in?' she says.

'Come this way, if you can manage it,' Patrick says, climbing back through the window. 'We didn't figure there was any point in digging out the doorway.'

Patrick disappears and Bill hoists Helen up onto the window ledge, groaning. Inside, she finds herself on the first-floor landing. There is a smell of smoke coming to her from below. As she descends, she notes a pattern of rectangles where the wallpaper is brighter. She traces the four edges of one of these with a finger: a ghostly facsimile of the family photo gallery.

She pauses at the foot of the stairs to get her breath, and Bill slips past her, following Patrick, giving her a squeeze on the shoulder. As her eyes adjust to the low light she sees that there is a pen and a pad by the phone. Pairs of trainers are arranged on a rack by the front door. The order of the place is eerie, as though the Bowyers have just popped out and might return at any moment to find this group of snowsuit-clad interlopers squatting in their home. She starts to imagine breaking into her own home, after she has left it, seeing herself in the third person, but she pushes the thought away.

Helen goes to the front room, which is darker and hazy with smoke. Patrick is saying something to Bill, but breaks off when he sees her. It's warm. Without saying anything she moves past Naomi, seated on the sofa, towards the fire, taking off her mittens to rub her hands. She turns and watches as Bill claps Patrick in his arms, slapping him on the back.

'Sorry about the smoke,' Patrick says. 'I cleared the chimney as best I could.'

'Where did you find wood?' Bill says.

'In one of the barns. It was a little wet. There were also a couple of dead cows, frozen stiff.'

'Says something about the Bowyers, to give up before they had even run out of wood. To leave their animals to die like that.'

Helen turns to face Naomi, who is sat with her arms wrapped around her knees. The poor girl is deathly pale. She is, ordinarily, in a constant state of fidgety exuberance, so – although it shouldn't come as a surprise – it's a shock to see her so deflated and still.

There is a reassuring tingling in Helen's toes, as feeling returns; the warmth of the fire at her back.

'How was the night?' she asks.

'Neither of us slept very much,' Naomi says. 'By the time we arrived it was pretty well dark, and the house was freezing. I kept expecting someone to come for us, for someone to have followed us.'

'What's happening in the village?' Patrick says.

'Helen went with Joe this morning to see Sandra, and Alan,' Bill says.

'How are they?'

Everyone turns to look at Helen. All she can think of is the approach to the farm. Those signs nailed to the trees. The hedgerows buried by the snow. Desolate, is the word that presents itself to her. 'I think it's best you stay away from them,' she says, and then, more gently, when she sees how Patrick quails – suddenly a boy again – with grief and guilt: 'They are going ahead with the funeral this afternoon.'

Bill puts a hand on Patrick's head. 'We should talk about what happens next. When we're going to leave.'

Naomi shifts in her seat, picks some lint off the arm of the sofa. 'We have talked about it.'

'Helen,' Patrick says, 'Dad just told me that you're coming along with us. And I was thinking. The halftracks will be arriving this afternoon. We could hitch a ride with them. In one, two days, we'd be at the exit point.' Naomi shifts again, crossing her legs. The nylon of her snowsuit squeaks against the cushion. Patrick continues: 'Naomi doesn't think it's safe.'

'I don't think we should go back to the village,' Naomi says.

'It's obvious that she's sick,' Patrick says, turning to Helen.

'Patrick,' Bill says.

'She's not going to be able to walk all the way to Harwich.'

'I don't want to be a burden,' Helen says. 'I have been feeling under the weather, a little confused, but I didn't realise that it was anything ... obvious.' The heat from the fire, the smoke. Helen realises that she feels a little faint. She looks over at Bill, his fists clenched, unclenching. He is saying something to Patrick but she doesn't catch it.

She reaches out for a chair and gasps as lightning forks along her spine and down the back of her legs; a white-hot, winnowing instant so intense that it can't be understood as a sensation, that makes it seem as if she is a thing made only of that single breath, and that afterwards leaves her nerves crackling and fizzing as her muscles spasm, throwing up their quaint defences against the outrage that has already swept past. Everyone has stopped talking and they are looking at her, that much she is aware of. But she has no idea how much time has passed since she spoke. The pain, when it comes, has this dilatory effect that makes it difficult to hold interest in the concerns of those around her, in the terrible events of the past couple of days – of the last twelve months in fact – and their unfolding consequences, because it seems impossible that time will ever resume its stately and previously unquestioned course. Then it subsides, and anxiety crashes in.

She thinks of the sheer force of her feelings when she first met David. When Joe was first born. How she felt love in her teeth, how it thrummed in her bones.

Bill is at her side asking if she is OK and she is nodding and patting his hand to buy herself a few beats to wait out the wave that is crashing over her, to fall back in step with those around her.

She looks around and Patrick has gone.

'He went to fetch more wood,' Naomi says.

Helen looks up at Bill. 'Go on, go after him. I'm OK.'

He squeezes her hand and pulls up his hood, going after Patrick, and leaving Helen alone with Naomi.

Naomi takes her phone from her pocket but the screen is black. She sighs, clasping it in her fist.

'Do you think we'll have another election?' Helen says, regaining composure.

Naomi looks over at her. She smiles and puts away her phone. 'What makes you ask?'

'I don't know. I was thinking about Nicky Bowyer, the woman who lived here. We were friends, once. About how she became a Tory. About how I hadn't really considered the fact that there might not be another election. Have you spoken to your parents? I seem to be asking everyone that today. I've come over all mother goose.' She takes a breath; now that the pain has passed, all her thoughts are rushing at once.

'Have I spoken to them today? Or just lately?'

'I just wondered how they were.'

'I didn't really feel like calling them to update them with the latest news.'

'No, of course. I didn't mean to . . .' Helen trails off. How careless, she thinks.

'Never mind,' Naomi says.

Helen tries again: 'Bill took the axe away. He's hidden it somewhere.'

'Well, thank god. I told Patrick to get rid, nagged him at what felt like every fucking step. Like I'm somehow safer with that thing in the house.'

Helen's eyes widen. Does she mean that she's worried Patrick would turn on her?

'No, no,' Naomi continues. 'I don't mean that – he could never – not to me. But he's so jumpy. Was pacing around upstairs all night, wearing out the floorboards, while I tried to sleep. Hefting that axe. And it made me so angry because, well, we're still doing it, aren't we? We're still talking about him.' She pauses, searching for the words. '*I* need someone to talk to. I need *someone* to ask me.'

Helen takes her in: her chest thrust forward, one arm extended, wrist bared – a posture that is both challenge and submission; one that demands: open my veins. Her head is cocked to one side and with her delicate nose, her fine golden hair, she looks like some tiny migratory bird at the end of a flight across the sea. Journey-worn but defiant. Helen wonders how many times Naomi has rehearsed this conversation in her mind since the events of yesterday, both in anger and contrition, just as she has rehearsed her conversation with Joe. But she doesn't say anything, and continues to polish the surface of the dining table with her tissue, working at an invisible stain. The question hangs in the air between them.

'Ask me whether he did it.' Naomi drops her hands to the table. 'You can't even look at me, can you? Ask me whether Ian raped me.'

The word uttered aloud makes everything – Ian's violence, Patrick's violence, her own cruelty – suddenly unbearably acute, so that she is embarrassed and wants to rush to make amends.

So she says: 'Naomi, my poor dove. I didn't ask because I didn't have to.'

'Didn't have to? What on earth do you mean didn't have to?'

'I didn't have to because of course – of *course* – I believe you.'

'I see. The thing is, I wasn't worried that you wouldn't believe me. I was worried that you wouldn't care.'

Helen holds her hands up; the fury coming off Naomi puts a shimmer into the air between them.

'And when I say wouldn't care,' Naomi continues, 'I mean wouldn't *do* anything. Not just you. All of you. You can't imagine, these past few days. All I have wanted. A word from any of you.'

This must be the point at which Naomi would have broken off in her rehearsals for this moment. Because what else could they have done, other than what Patrick has already done? No one – Helen least of all – wanted to think about how these things would have taken care of themselves before the snow. She does not want to accept that the world has changed. It has been easy, until now, to let something like forgetting, closer to obscuring, fall over her. So easy that its slow accretion has gone unnoticed. She has carried on living in that world of emergency services and wigs and gavels and gowns, of next-day delivery and diagnoses, of care for the careworn and opportunities for the newly born. All the while the disaster has been unfolding.

Now that Naomi is standing before her, bright with hurt, her failings are clear. She holds out her hands and an arrow of pain arcs a lightning span down her right side. Naomi takes them, dry-eyed.

'They are going to kill us, you realise that?'

'Why on earth would they do that?'

'When they realise that there will be no flashing lights, no day in court – they'll turn on us.'

'Naomi, we've known these people our entire lives, how could you possibly imagine—'

'Helen,' she interrupts, 'how can you not? After what happened yesterday, how can you not imagine?'

She doesn't know what to say. She tries to conceive of feelings so strong they could make you pick up an axe and hack someone to death. When Joe was first born she was constantly stalked by a feeling that she could crush him – simply squeeze the life out of him. The most she feels now is shifts in awareness, like coming back to your body when you have spent too long in the bath, and the water has begun to cool.

Something has now, finally, shifted. Her feelings – her sympathy for Naomi, which now floods her chest – were forestalled by her unexamined expectations about what would happen. Reality is becoming increasingly porous with each passing day. She has lived her life under a set of certainties that never revealed themselves to her until now, too late.

'All I know,' she finally says, 'is that I am sorry. That I couldn't stop it. This isn't your fault, Naomi' – Helen regrets these words for their cinematic cliché; their self-evident nature – 'you have to know that.'

Patrick comes in, his arms full of logs. He pauses in the doorway and looks at them each in turn.

'These are a little drier, found 'em in the other barn. Had to manoeuvre around the cows.'

Patrick dumps the logs by the fire and throws a couple on top, stirring the embers. Helen enjoys the pop and crackle of the bark, and is grateful for the excuse it gives them all for their silence.

Bill follows on soon after, panting, depositing more logs onto the pile.

'These should keep you warm until this evening,' he says, slapping his hands together. It seems as though something has been decided, between Patrick and Bill.

'I still think it's a bad idea,' Naomi says. 'For us to come back to the village.'

'What other choice is there?' Patrick says.

To leave Helen behind. That is the other choice; to start to walk north without her. Thankfully, Naomi doesn't voice it. Bill sits and they all stare into the fire. After a few moments, by silent accord, Helen and Bill begin to gather themselves up.

'We'll see you later.' He places a hand on Patrick's cheek and hugs him. Helen squeezes Naomi's shoulder. She hopes that she has provided some comfort to her. She is going to need Naomi, as much as Naomi needs her now, when they embark on whatever comes next.

It has stopped snowing. They retrace their steps. The sled bumps over the tracks they made on the way out, now frozen into scooped troughs and miniature ravines. The pain returns.

She feels unable to sit upright so she stares up at the ash-grey clouds, listening to the thrum of the generator, its rising volume announcing to her their approach to the village.

She wakes, once again being carried in Bill's arms. He places her on the bed and lies down beside her. His breath tickles her ear. She wants to tell Bill about what passed between her and Naomi, but she is so tired that she can't find the words. And the warmth of the bed, the feel of Bill's breath on her skin, is so gorgeous that her desire to preserve the moment wins out.

'I need a holiday,' she says.

'We should get some sleep,' he says, sighing deeply and closing his eyes. 'We're going to need as much energy as we can muster for the next few days.'

'Do you think that Patrick will be able to forgive himself?' she says.

'Forgive himself? He hasn't accepted that what he did is wrong.'

Helen lets his words hang in the air for a moment; she wants to ask what passed between them in the barn, but knows she should give him some time to process it. 'In any case, you're going to have to forgive him,' she says. 'I know that much.'

'Can a person just commit a murder and then get on with their life?'

She wonders at what point Ian might have realised that Patrick was being serious, that it wasn't all a joke.

The kind of forgiveness she imagined as she spoke was less transformative and more immediate. A churchy tea-morning type forgiveness. Doilies and stale gingernuts.

He turns onto his side and drapes an arm across her chest. She feels a stirring of desire as she inhales the sleepy smell of him, as his weight settles into her, and it catches her off guard. She is full of the soft-focus clarity this feeling brings. It is unfair that she should have this window now when, really, she should be sleeping.

Helen runs her hands over the smooth skin of her distended belly. It feels alien and unbodily and makes her think of the time that she and Bill had watched porn together. She had suggested it, only half wanting to and daring him to say no. They settled into the bed with his laptop. She was curious to see what he would choose but he stopped at the first page, his index finger hovering over the track pad. She reached over and clicked on a random thumbnail and the video that opened was of a woman squatting and pissing all over the floor. The tension between them snapped and they laughed, gratefully, but neither of them moved to turn it off. There was someone off camera, speaking, but it wasn't loud enough to make out what they were saying. Bill had said something about how lonely you would have to be to seek out a video of a woman pissing – to have been excluded from such incidental intimacies. The woman's body was not as pristine and artificially contoured as Helen had expected. She was lean and her skin was blotchy and something about the way the light caught the downy hairs on her forearms made Helen well up with feeling, as though someone was pressing their palm against her sternum. When the woman finished pissing she stood up and a man's arse appeared from the right-hand side of the shot. Helen closed the laptop before anything else could happen, pulling Bill's face towards hers.

JOE

'Fuck,' Joe says, laughing gently to himself. 'Fuuuuuuuck.'

He blows out his cheeks. He wraps his arms around his chest and spins in a circle and jumps and shouts, a lilting melody: 'FuUUuuuuuuck me.'

Rachel smiles over her shoulder, clapping her hands together and rubbing their sides. 'We should get moving, I'm getting cold.'

Joe knows that he must be cold too. But in this moment, he doesn't feel it. Looking at her, Joe tries to picture their child, but immediately rebukes himself for the possibility he might jinx it, so early on, when things are so uncertain. He can't remember the last time he saw a baby. They were first to be evacuated and there hasn't been a birth in the village since the snow started.

They walk towards the lower end of the playing fields, towards the bridge over the railway tracks that will take them to the estate and then to the quay. For the first time in six months he unconsciously pats his right pocket for his phone, urged by that old instinct to test any momentous revelation against the rub of other events, to contextualise it against food photos from friends he has fallen out of touch with and headlines about election corruption in countries he will never visit. It is only now that he feels how small his world has become: now that it isn't large enough to contain this piece of news.

He wants to tell his mum, to hold the news up to her like a school report card. Before he knows it, they have reached the bottom of the fields. There is no way that he can face the pyre at the quay in his current state, no way that he could summon anything like the appropriate solemnity for anyone who might be loitering there, anyone he might meet along the way. He stops in his tracks and looks over towards the playground, half-turns towards its gateway.

'Rachel?'

She stops and spins around theatrically. 'It's a little cold to stop and play on the swings, Joe.'

He laughs. 'I need a minute, I think. Go on, go to the Nottage. Phone your mum. I'll see you at home.'

She waves as she turns, and disappears behind the hedgerow leading to the railway bridge.

Only the tops of the monkey bars and the climbing frame, still visible, give any sense of what the place was. The bench under the horse chestnut tree where he would sit with his dad and eat ice creams is completely buried. He curls his fingers in his gloves and can feel the cool, smooth surface of a conker in his sweating palm. Did his dad feel like this when he found out that he was on the way? Did he feel superpowered? Like he could flip cars nose over tail?

He doesn't think that it's possible. He used to sit and stare at the paintings of his dad's, still hung around the house long after he had left, until his eyes blurred. Shapes would emerge and then disappear. They told him nothing. Worse than that, they threw him back on himself, to bathe in projections of his own anxieties. Green threads of slick acrylic that became snakes as thick as his wrist, and jaundiced patches of yellow that erupted into barn-high fires. He came to hate the cruelty of abstraction and its insistent, singular message of: you! It's all your fault!

What in the fuck had he been doing before today? He had just been waiting, he supposes, for something – for anything – to happen.

Joe clambers onto the platform of the climbing frame and squats on his haunches. It's stultifying, living in this world of partial abstractions created by the snow. With nothing to do, he's been spending all of his time stuck in a cycle of nostalgia.

He takes a deep breath and steadies himself, feeling his heart-rate slow. He jumps down from the climbing frame. The shadows are short now and the sun on the snow is making him blink and shade his eyes. It must be almost midday.

On the bridge across the railway tracks he pauses and peers over the side, as he always did as a child. The overhead cables have snapped in the cold and hang limply from the masts. At school they had a special assembly where they watched a video, one of those from the eighties with bombastic voice-overs and kids walking around with tape cassette Walkmans, in which a young lad with a fishing rod is killed because his trailing line catches the overhead wires and electrocutes him. A grizzled bloke from the railways stood next to the TV while it played and answered questions afterwards, telling a whole host of stories about people's skin catching fire and their blood boiling.

This video, and another one about the dangers of chip pan fires which was brought in by the part-time fireman who rode around the village on a motorbike, are the only two instances

Joe can remember being prepared for the specific dangers of adulthood. They seem quite esoteric now.

There is a man plodding along the track, pulling a sled with a tarp stretched over it behind him. The snot frozen in his greying moustache catches in the midday sun. Joe doesn't recognise him. He waves.

'What's the name of this place?' the man calls up.

Joe points to the station signs lining the platform. 'Wivenhoe.'

'One more to tick off the list, then.'

'Headed to the exit point?'

'Where else?'

'Right you are.'

They consider each other for a moment. The man stoops to tighten one of the ropes securing the tarp. He has a strange habit of blowing out his cheeks and whistling. Pheewweee.

'Going to make a go of it alone?'

'Got my Freedom Pass in my back pocket.' He slaps his thigh with an open palm, scattering powder. He pulls up one of the earflaps of his trapper hat. 'Say, I can hear a generator. Is there anywhere holding supplies around here?'

'We have a little depot set up on the quay, not far. We're waiting on a delivery – supposed to come today, in fact – so there might not be much. But happy to take you there, for what it's worth.'

'If it's no bother?'

'No bother, I'm headed back that way.'

The man turns back and pulls his sled up onto the train station platform and they meet on the road, falling into step alongside one another.

'Seen anything along the way?' Joe says.

'Like what? Polar bears?'

'No, I was thinking more along the line of . . .' Joe pauses, but he draws a blank. 'Actually I don't know what, come to think of it.'

'Heard the rumours about the bears. Spotted some strange tracks a while back, but no bears. No roaming bands of feral murderous teenagers either. Just a few lonely old men like myself.'

'What made you wait so long?'

'My wife.' He coughs and clears his throat.

'I see. I'm sorry.'

'Don't be. She's with God now. More than can be said for the two of us.'

The man produces a flask from inside his snowsuit and takes a gulp, pouring out a little onto the snow. 'Pheewweee.'

They round the corner onto the high street and walk in reflective silence for a couple of minutes. Joe is aware of curtains twitching at the corner of his vision: people drawn to their windows by the whispering grind of the blades of the loaded sled cutting through the powder and gliding over the ice below. Being seen walking down the high street at the side of a grockle today – especially one so freshly arrived – might serve to add to the general air of paranoia. But fuck them. He is taking great pleasure in holding the secret of his new knowledge in the company of a stranger.

'So what's the situation like, up there? In the city,' Joe says.

'Pretty well the same as it is just here. Covered in snow.' The man laughs: a whistling, wheezing sound, his back arched and his head flung back, the sound echoing along the naked faces of the houses, before shaking his head with some huge gravity that pays fatherly respect to the universe in all its recal-citrant ironies. 'For the most part people have been leaving,' he continues. 'A few chancers stayed behind to loot people's houses and from the shopping centres, but when they realised there was nothing doing, they scarpered too. Can't hardly sell stolen TVs to one another now, can they? But, as it goes, lately the tide has turned back the other way. Three days ago as I was setting out I noticed that one of the office buildings over by Canary Wharf was lit up like a Christmas tree. Blue lights and solar panels all up one side. They were dragging sacks of soil up the side using ropes. Bloody mad if you ask me. Some point you have to accept that you're licked. You thinking of heading back that way?'

'Hadn't considered it,' Joe says. 'I was just curious. Think we'll have much weather today?'

'Shouldn't hope so. Think I might make the exit point by tomorrow evening if this keeps up.'

'I could see it.'

By now they have reached the bottom of the road leading down the quay. The Nottage is off to the right; Joe can see a few pairs of snowshoes hanging on the hooks (the last thing he needs right now would be to get cornered by Reg). Home is to the left. And ahead, the river.

'Just in there, ask for the vicar.' Joe points.

The man smiles and taps the side of his head with a mitten. 'I'll follow my lugholes.'

They face one another, hands at their sides; the awkward uncertainty of the parting of fresh acquaintance. Joe is in no rush to speed things along, to get to the task that awaits him.

'Well,' the man continues, 'standing here chewing the

92

proverbial with you all day isn't going to get me anywhere.' He stows his flask away and stoops to check his tarpaulin. 'Pleasant as it is.'

'Right you are,' Joe says. 'Was nice to meet you.'

'Be lucky,' the man says.

'Yeh, look after yourself.'

The man bows his head, running the slack of the sled line through his palms until it goes taut and the sled begins to slice its way through the snow behind him.

Joe starts towards the river course, but then hesitates and turns.

'I'm going to be a dad,' he calls. His voice sounds distant, not his own, too quiet. Away from the canyon of houses, his words are swallowed up by the wind and snow. The man doesn't respond. So, he tries again: 'I'm going to be a dad, I just found out.'

The man stops and turns back, the sled sliding to a stop against his calf. A huge smile crosses his face. 'Pheeeewweeeeeeeee. That's wonderful. It's wonderful news. Wonderful.'

Joe has the strange empty feeling of the tail end of an adrenaline rush. His teeth chatter and he finds he can't say anything else. He is frozen in place, laughing like a loon.

'What's your name, son?'

'Joe.'

'Be lucky, Joe.'

The man continues on. Joe wants to call him back again, to delay the task of moving Ian's body, but he has nothing left to say.

The upturned dinghy is nestled between two mounds – submerged pleasure yachts. A fresh smattering of snow now partially conceals the disturbance they made. As he approaches, he is filled with a certain kind of dread he last felt approaching a mouse caught in a trap, certain that at any moment it would jump up and thrash around.

He steels himself and hoists the boat up and over onto its side, his feet slipping as he tries to find purchase in the uneven snow. He exhales a sigh of relief to find the body as they left it, wrapped and weighted on the sled. So scared was he that it might have moved or been nibbled at by a fox or rat that he hadn't stopped to think how he might feel to be confronted by the evidence of Patrick's original violence against Ian's body.

He checks the tarp is secure and takes up the rope, pulling the sled free. It sticks, the blades having frozen slightly, and then comes free, shooting out between the two boats and almost knocking him over. It's heavier than Joe remembers from yesterday and he finds himself comparing the weight of it to pulling his mum up to Sandra's earlier in the day, before he can stop himself.

Having cleared the boats and made it onto the frozen river he turns back towards the Nottage. No one loitering. The grockle's sled is secured outside. A window opens on the quayside and a woman leans out. She yells something but Joe only catches the last word: 'SHAME'. The woman near enough spits it. The window slams closed again. Joe feels sick. The last thing he needs, at this point, is an audience. He wants to present Ian's body on the pyre as a fait accompli to the village. Any opportunity for everyone to gather together and ruminate, aside from the funeral, will only increase the chance of summary justice. If that starts, will they stop with Patrick? No point in considering that any further just now, so he presses on.

There is guilt. It's hardly a fitting departure for someone so young: hauled across the ice under a tarpaulin. Circumstances have dispensed with so much ceremony since the snow began.

By the time he reaches the pyre, his toes are numb but he is sweating and thirsty. The taste of sherry and spent adrenaline in the back of his throat. With nothing to halt its progress the wind whips mercilessly across the ice, catching the powder in swirls and eddies. It dries his lips and makes his eyes water and sting.

He drops the sled rope and turns, easing his back. The quay, and the village behind, are spread out in front of him. It's an alpine, chocolate-box scene from this vantage. Picturesque but alien to him. The utter transformation is so much clearer from the outside, looking in.

Off to his right, heading towards the quay from the direction of the marshes, he spots a man pulling a sled, on which a figure lies supine. Bill, towing his mum; he can tell by the colour of the snowsuits.

A peal of laughter reaches him, carried on the wind above the noise of the generator. Rachel, fastening her snowshoes outside the Nottage, talking to the grockle. They walk together to the road that leads up to the village, where the man turns and walks into the lane. Joe relishes watching Rachel at a distance, in a way that makes him aware of the fact that they have been spending too much time together, no space between them to allow familiarity to relapse and renew.

The wind calls him to task, lashing his face and making him gasp. He gets down on one knee and tries to hoist the body over his shoulder but it is totally stiff. Instead, he stands and drags the sled closer to the pyre.

Joe takes one last glance back towards the quay, to check that he is unobserved. The logs are stacked to just above his knees.

If he gets Ian half on then he can lever his legs up. He tries to put aside all thoughts of the boy he grew up with, the man he lived alongside – as he skirts the pyre and reaches over the top, gripping the tarpaulin at the point where he guesses Ian's armpits are. The plastic slips against his mittens; he readjusts and his fingers find some purchase. He heaves, and with one tug manages to get the rigid cocoon half up and onto the platform. He takes a breath and skirts back to the other side, lifting the other end from the sled and swinging it around.

As it settles into place a gust of wind catches a corner of the plastic. It flaps free and reveals an arm, a hand, ghostly white and sheened with gore. Joe falls backwards on the snow as if stung. He swallows, and jumps to secure the corner of the tarp under the weight of Ian's body. He closes his eyes, presses them into the heels of his hands until the image, seared onto his retinas, begins to fade.

Then he turns and starts to make his way across the ice, towards the house.

HELEN

She smells acrid, just-caught currants and orange peel and plays her fingers through the tight curls of hair on Bill's chest. There is a party-ring, late-afternoon, post-crash-nap sickly-sweet-cut-with-iron taste under her tongue. Has she slept? She must have, because she has the dream-drugged sense that she has won the lottery. Which, now she thinks about it, is surely not possible. She takes a deep breath that washes these feelings down through her chest, where they settle into place among the sedimentary guilt of her impending departure.

Is someone baking a cake? This also does not seem possible. But as the rush of the lottery win fades, the smell of burnt sugar lingers.

She craves sweet things all the time now. Fresh strawberries and hand-whipped cream like the ones she would top Joe's birthday cake with every year. She could eat a whole bowl of trifle with her hands. Eat jam from the jar. Except when she is actually presented with food she can't eat and she wants to throw the food across the room in frustration.

The cake recipe is probably still pinned on the board by the phone under last year's calendar. She used to sit at the counter every Christmas with a cup of tea and transfer the important dates over to a new calendar. Birthdays and deaths. That kitchen is a graveyard of useless things now. But why throw them out?

Bill is still sleeping. The tip of his tongue pokes between his teeth and his little nose-hairs are quivering with his breath. David's nose-hair disgusted her but Bill's has always made her want to grab up handfuls of him. It's curious. She has never been one of those people who likes squeezing other people's spots – she had to do a lot of that kind of thing, draining bed sores and the like, when she was nursing – but there was also some relationship between what she found disgusting and what she found comforting, and that distance has shortened. Perhaps it comes from spending a lot more time in bed.

All sensations that shelter her from the erasure of pain are comforting. Her thoughts forking in this direction make her bite Bill's ear.

'Owww,' he grumbles. 'What's that for?'

'Oh I don't know.'

'Mmmmm.'

'Can you smell cake?'

'I can smell cake.'

'Why would they be baking?'

'I don't know, Helen.'

'You're awake now. We may as well go downstairs.'

'Let me sleep. A little longer.'

She bites his ear again.

'Nmmmmmmmm.'

'Well, I'm hardly going to go down there on my own.'

She lets the threat hang in the air. She's all talk. But she can still smell those currants, and it's stronger now and making her hungry in the way she knows is all talk too. This pull, of arrival and departure, has been torturing her all day, all year. When Joe was a toddler he was very fussy about his food. Fish fingers and lasagne. Grated carrot and apple. There wasn't much else that he would go for.

David would always try to play the aeroplane game – open wide! here comes the jumbo jet – but it just made Joe cry. He kept trying, as though it was some kind of indictment against him as a parent that he couldn't get Joe to take to it.

That was David's problem; it wasn't that he couldn't pay attention – or wasn't willing to – it was more that he focused on the wrong thing. Like when they were redecorating this bedroom when he first moved in and they were getting ready for Joe to arrive and they got into a raging argument about the skirting boards. Before they had even chosen the paint, before they had chosen the curtains.

He is probably in an artists' camp now, with views of the Mediterranean. Telling some Italian woman that she has under-seasoned the bolognese. Helen is surprised to find that this thought generates no bitterness, and is a force of habit. It is somehow concerning, and she hopes she is not becoming magnanimous.

A little while after David left her for the final time (or she supposed, as he sees it, when she finally left him, because she stopped apologising for her existence after every senseless row), when she was selling Avon for some extra money – or for the idea of some extra money, because the extra money never actually materialised – she visited the house of a woman who, it was commonly known, had been left by her husband but hadn't yet accepted the fact. It was the day that Nelson Mandela was released from prison and she had the Radio 4 report on, which played throughout Helen's visit, while she unpacked lipsticks, eye palettes and samples of a line of body products that the US Army had apparently ordered in huge bulk after it was accidentally discovered to have incidental mosquito-repelling qualities, talking the woman through payment plans that she didn't need because she was extremely wealthy, applying blusher samples to the back of her hand to demonstrate its quality. The woman kept just saying: it's so wonderful, it's so wonderful – did you hear? did you hear? And refilling her glass of white wine. Raising her glass and toasting Freedom. Until eventually she burst into tears and sobbed that her husband had left her, leaving Helen to wonder why in every aspect of her life she was expected to care – to attend to the needs of every person that she came into contact with, to throw herself, every day, into that insatiable, widening maw – and why this woman's pain, when it finally revealed itself, made Helen feel a rush of disgust at her own. She was a soap-opera cliché of the spurned woman, a tornado of Chardonnay and Chanel No. 5, and what was worse was she was *rich*: it was a privileged pain – a vision of what Helen desperately wanted to avoid becoming, enabled by the thing that she wanted – needed – so badly that Helen found herself screaming: stop this, stop right now and pull yourself together! while she relived the moment that very morning when all of the cards she had dumped into the river the night before, every one that David had ever written her, were nosed back in by the advancing tide to be deposited in the mud, making a sad trail from the pub back towards the house which—

'Helen?'

Her tongue is beached against the roof of her mouth. Her eyes are heavy.

'We going downstairs then?' Bill says, as he's pulling on a pair of socks. 'I have to say, the smell of that cake is hard to ignore.'

Did she scream at that horrid woman? It's fading. She has a competing memory of turning on the kettle and making tea, of managing to sell a few measly lipsticks. She knows that she threw David's cards in the river, and that the woman avoided her after that day. Was it out of a sense of embarrassment for Helen, a worry that she would try and sell her more products? Or a sense of shame at her pain: that she was no better, no more loved than Helen, with her product case. Worse: that she had exposed her pain to the Avon lady. Oh, who cares. Why did she ever care about any of it? Bill is humming a Van Morrison tune as he straightens his socks. Are they really going to leave all this?

'Come on then, old bird.'

'Sqwaaaar.'

He gets down on one knee and pulls her legs around, helps her drop them down over the edge, pressing his fingers in the arches of her feet.

'You, my brown-eyed girl.'

'Me?'

'Yoouu, my, my brown-eyed girl.'

'You missed your calling, crooner.'

'Don't I know it. Come on, heave-ho' – he pulls her to her feet and slowly waltzes her over to the dressing table and back – 'do you remember when?'

'Less, day by day.'

He laughs, singing: 'Sha la la la la la la la la la la la la.'

'Let's go and see about that cake.'

'May as well bring the bags down.'

'Leave mine, until I've spoken to Joe.'

In the kitchen, they find Rachel huddled over the cooker. Bill drops his bag on the floor.

'That smells good,' Helen says.

'Oh!' Rachel jumps and spins round, a wooden skewer in her hand. 'You made me jump. It's almost done.' She opens the oven and puts the tin back inside. 'Fruit cake. My mum's recipe.'

'Hi, Mum, how you feeling?' Joe says.

'Where did you get the fruit?' Helen asks.

'I've been saving it. Just currants and apricots. I thought we could all do with something to cheer us up.'

The steam from the oven, the smell of caught currants, the house full of people, the snow at the window – Helen has a fleeting festive feeling that is totally at odds with the events of the day. She considers asking Rachel what possessed her to bake a cake, but something in the brittle brightness of her manner stops her; makes her think she'll find out soon enough.

'Since we're using the gas,' she says, glancing at Bill, 'shall we make some tea?'

'I'll fill the kettle.'

Helen and Rachel sit at the table with Joe and watch Bill as he pours meltwater from the tank by the window into the kettle.

'How are they?' Joe says. 'Patrick and Naomi.'

'I think they had a pretty rough night,' Helen says.

'Long night of the soul,' Bill mutters, staring down at the kettle.

'The signs that Nicky Bowyer had up on the farm,' Helen says, shaking her head. 'Disgraceful.'

'She was still there?' Joe asks, incredulous.

'No, no. Long gone.' She thinks again of the ghostly family gallery lining the stairway and feels a pang of guilt.

'So, then. Did you ask Patrick about what happened?' Rachel says.

Helen looks over towards Bill, his fists on the counter, squared around the stove. His head drops, ever so slightly. She is glad that someone else has asked this of him, so that she doesn't have to.

The kettle whistles and he pours out the tea. Rachel goes to the cooker and takes out the cake, releasing a cloud of sweet steam. She prods it once more and, satisfied, brings it to the table. Bill passes out the mugs and they sit in silence waiting for him to begin.

'We did speak a bit. Didn't have long, mind.' He pauses, gathering his thoughts. 'Well, obviously I asked him what the hell he was thinking. Asked what the hell came over him. He said that when Naomi told him what had happened to her, what Ian had done, he was angry. Of course he was. Furious. Who wouldn't be?' He looks up from his mug for confirmation, the support he needs to go on. They all nod, and he continues: 'So, at first he thought he would just go and speak to him. Not to *do* anything. Just talk. But then, when he started thinking about what he might say, he just got more and more angry. Started to go a little crazy. He should have talked to Naomi, but he couldn't. He knew he would be making it worse, with this fury, bringing it to her. Making it all about him and about *his* feelings.'

He pauses, drinks his tea, grimacing. 'All of this we had already been over; night before last when he was here at the house. I said that he shouldn't speak to Ian. He was too upset. No good would come of it. I thought I had got through to him.

'After, he went round to Naomi's. Told me they couldn't look at one another. He started to feel that – well, you would, wouldn't you? – he starts to feel that it's his fault, that he should have stopped it. It plays on his mind: why hadn't he ever had a word with him? With Ian, about how he looks at her, the way he's always looked at her. We've all seen it.' He stops again; this time

Joe and Rachel are staring at the table. Helen squeezes Bill's hand, nods, willing him to continue. 'But then he knows he's just doing the same thing. Making it about his feelings over hers, so he just gets angrier and *angrier*. So yesterday morning he decides to go for a walk, to try and give her some space.' He stops, swallows. 'By this point I wanted to shake the boy because for goodness sake what she needed him to do was be there. But he's stalking about. He's picked up the axe; thought he might split some logs to let some of the fire trapped in his belly out. He's walking up the high street, headed to the woods, when he spots him. Ian. Strolling casual as you like. And then ... well, you know what happened next. He said there was a smell like ozone. Like a new car. And the next thing he knew, Ian was dead at his feet. Everyone running out across the ice from the quayside. Blood on the snow.'

Bill takes another sip from his tea, more tentative this time. He is breathing deeply. Helen wants to offer some words of comfort, or at least say something to draw focus, to give him time to recover.

'Why didn't he talk to us? That's what I asked him, again and again. Yes, he told me about what had happened. He told me he was angry. But when he couldn't speak to Naomi why didn't he come home? Why didn't he come home?'

The question hangs unanswered. Unanswerable. Everyone has averted their eyes but no one moves. Helen thinks, for a moment, of the scene in their bedroom only fifteen minutes ago and wonders how such lightness was possible. An atmosphere of unreality has hung over the house since the snow began. Over the village, and no doubt the country. With the future so uncertain, time doesn't move forward but piles up; each day, each moment inscribed on top of one another in a ceaseless, sutured present that makes cause and effect strangers to one another.

'I spoke to Naomi,' Helen says, much more quietly than she intends. 'While you were in the barn with Patrick. She's livid. Furious with us for not asking *her* whether Ian had attacked her.'

'Well, of course we believed her,' Bill says.

'What did we do about it, though?'

They fall silent once again.

'God, what a mess,' Rachel finally says, taking up the knife and cutting into the cake. 'I imagine no one will feel like eating this now but, since I've made it . . .' She pauses, knife pointed at the ceiling.

'I'll have some,' Joe says. 'Thanks, babe.'

Helen smiles assent at Rachel and squeezes Bill's hand, pulling him from his stupor so that he mumbles the same. She cuts two generous slices and passes them across the table.

'Just one last thing,' Joe says, laying down his fork with care next to his untouched cake. 'Everything is ready for the funeral. I moved Ian onto the pyre. We set it up exactly as before. Thing is, I don't think either of you should come.'

Helen sees the sense in this, yet: 'I should be there for Sandra.'

'Joe is right, Helen,' Bill says. 'We'll only make matters worse.' The relief is plain on Joe's face: one less battle to fight. 'Did you see the halftrack? When you were out on the river?' Bill continues.

'No. I couldn't hear anything either, though I was close to the generator. I guess they must still be at least a few hours out if they haven't rounded the creek yet. When are you leaving, Bill?'

Before Helen has even thought about it the plate is falling. It hits the tiles and breaks clean down the middle. Joe pushes his chair back and bends down and picks up the two pieces, placing them on the table.

'I'm sorry, I wasn't paying attention,' she says. 'I had a pain, in my arm.'

Joe is sweeping the crumbs with one hand into the other.

'Don't worry,' Rachel says and smiles across at her while she massages this phantom pain in her upper arm.

The plate is one of the Churchill blue willow saucers she bought the Christmas after David moved in. A willow arching over a lake, on which a boat sits. Two doves circle one another above – the crack now splitting them neatly in two, never to meet. Their first set of plates. The house still contains so many imprints of their time together. Far more, in fact, than of her relationship with Bill, which is longer and more full with love, but which saw less firsts. You don't buy a new set of dinner plates just because a new man moves in. Bill bought a lot of things for her the first few years they were together – Christmases and birthdays – but his taste is terrible. The dark corners of the house, cupboards, hard-to-access bookcases are full of coloured glass boots and brightly coloured Spanish bowls that Helen has secreted away.

First kiss first fuck first place first plates first son which sends her looping back to the past which summons Joe again and again in which she never leaves. She should tell him now, that she is leaving too, and break the loop. But she can't. She won't.

She wishes she could wear her wedding dress one more time. That was one first with Bill. David had said: anarchists don't get married. But it's in the loft, buried under her wonderful husband's awful kitsch, his magpie hoard.

Joe is at her side.

'We're going up for a rest,' he says.

JOE

Joe stares up from the bed at the galaxy of fluorescent stars that he stuck on the ceiling when he was twelve, and has never bothered to take down. The snow's arrival has made for some pretty great star gazing. On a clear night the Milky Way belts the sky with a kind of mist, you crick your neck trying to see all of the colours. The only light pollution is from the docks at Harwich, a huge firefly plume at the mouth of the estuary.

Rachel stirs, mumbles, and settles once again. As soon as they lay down she fell straight to sleep. Though he can feel an undertow of exhaustion, he has been too wired for anything aside from staring at the ceiling.

He considers his room and wonders where they might put a cot. He would have liked to have marked the baby's arrival in the time-honoured way, by spending an enormous amount of money on new things. Instead, he supposes that he will have to take a cot from one of the abandoned houses.

About three months ago he and Alfie had walked into town along the river. They had been trying to cultivate a couple of weed plants and some mushrooms in a spare bedroom in Alfie's house. He had found a grow kit and some seeds he bought online before the snow, and had completely forgotten about. It was nigh on impossible because of the temperature. There was a massive B&Q on the river at the edge of town and they thought there might still be something that they could salvage for their horticultural project. The Tesco opposite had been rinsed but Joe reasoned people might not have been thinking so much about gardening, or painting and decorating. He was wrong, of course; he hadn't considered that, aside from decorating supplies, it had everything an enterprising survivalist might need – tools, batteries, gas, insulation. It had been ransacked.

But just inside the door, there was a display that was intact. A banner that read GET READY FOR THE SUN! above a set of garden furniture: a cast iron table and chairs next to a gleaming gas grill and plastic pot plants, all underlain by lurid-green Astroturf – a catalogue image for a summer barbecue that never arrived.

They had sat down at the table – giddily hysterical at the absurdity of it – and had a make-believe tea party with watering can teapots and plantpot cups. Then they each grabbed one of the huge trolleys and raced each other around the darkened aisles, the tools and paint cans catching the light from their mobile phone torches. When they tired of this, they searched the aisles for fertiliser and compost before realising it would have been stored in the open-air yard behind the shop, and was therefore under several feet of snow.

They left empty-handed, but not really disappointed, having chased off their boredom.

They decided to continue on, up the hill to Colchester town centre, and didn't encounter another soul. All the way along, the windows were smashed. Some seemingly quite recently, shards of safety glass winking in the snow. There were piles of clothes at intervals, dusted with white, where they had been dragged from the shops and then abandoned. It was a strange scene, the destruction so systematic. It had a certain artfulness, all these useless things piled up – like an installation. It made Joe think of his dad, and his art. All his paintings were failed attempts at the scene in front of him; he never managed to make chaos signify more than the fact of its ugliness.

They poked their heads into a few of the shops, cautious archaeologists. In the British Heart Foundation every surface had been stripped, aside from the bookshelves, which were still crammed with paperbacks. Neither of them had a word to say to each other. They descended the hill back to the river and walked back home along the path.

'A cake,' Rachel says, rolling on to her back with a groan. 'A sodding cake. What was I thinking? Bill is sat at the table choking back his sobs and I bring over a fruit cake.'

'The cake was delicious. It should be celebrated. You should be celebrated. This should be celebrated. Whatever else has happened in the past couple of days.'

He inhales the sweet and sour smell of Rachel's skin and runs his fingers along the curve of her pelvis, over the gentle slope of her belly. She bats his hand away.

'That tickles' – yawning – 'creep.'

'How big do you reckon it is, right now?'

'Small, smaller than a pea.'

'What were you dreaming about?'

'Work. The kind of dream that I used to wake up from feeling all anxious. Now it just makes me miss it.'

Joe never remembers his dreams. He only ever carries an

emotional weather with him through to wakefulness. He can't believe that there is any significance to them.

'What would you have said,' Rachel says, 'to Patrick? If he had come home yesterday instead of going out for that walk and running into Ian on the high street.'

Joe can think of a hundred things that he would have said yesterday. He should have said that Ian was a piece of shit. That he shouldn't give him the satisfaction. That more violence would be the last thing Naomi would want.

'I would have tried to draw him out. Get him to talk. He can't have wanted it to get this far.'

They've always had an awkward relationship, he and Patrick. Brothers, but the same year in school. Competitors for their respective parent's affections. Adversaries on those rare occasions his mum and Bill fought, he standing with his mum and Patrick with his dad. Patrick always had a slight starriness about him that other lads punished him for. He paid attention to things that everyone else ignored. Like you might catch him making a daisy chain by the football goals. He sang with a little too much feeling in assembly. And when he did get caught he'd lash out. Quick to anger to defend his gentleness. An unhappy way of being that made Joe keep a certain distance.

It makes him think: what if this baby of his is a boy? Humiliation and anger, anger and humiliation; how will he find a way of directing his son's life away from this grim axis, from a lifetime spent shuffling from one pole to another? And if she's a girl? He can't bring himself to think about the attack on Naomi. He wants to put the thought of this baby away until he can think of it as something other than a victim or a perpetrator.

When he tries to imagine what was going through Patrick's head in those moments that his memory has erased, Joe's mind is completely blank. He simply can't. But he can imagine every moment that led up to Patrick finding himself on the high street. The rage, and the self-hatred inside it.

'Would you want me to do the same?' he says. 'To Ian.'

She sits up, pulling the cover up around her chest, her breath steaming. 'It's like everyone has been hit over the head. What kind of question is that?'

'I'm sorry,' he says. 'It's just, I feel as though all of us knew that this was going to happen, that all of us could have done something to stop it. But nobody did. Which makes me wonder whether I would have done the same.'

'You asking me that question, what I am hearing is: this is Naomi's fault. Her fault that Ian raped her. Her fault that Patrick killed Ian, that he did it for her.'

'No, of course I don't think that . . . none of this is Naomi's fault. That's not what I meant. Don't twist my words.'

'What did you mean then? That if Patrick had asked Naomi whether he should go after Ian, then somehow what did he is right?'

'What would you have wanted me to do?'

'What use is that kind of revenge in a place like this? Where she'd have to see his parents every time she goes to collect anything from the Nottage? Where all there is for anyone to do is nurture their resentments? He put his pride first.'

'You're right,' Joe says. Rachel is shaking her head, beginning to shiver and casting her eyes around the room for more layers. 'You are. But still. What was he supposed to do?'

'He shouldn't have killed him. There is no two ways about it.'

'And you, what would you have said to him, if you'd had the chance?'

'Think about Naomi. I'd have told him to think about her first. His feelings, his anger – they're all secondary. Or at least, they were, until he did what he did.'

Rachel's head twitches towards the window, and a moment later Joe hears it: church bells. The funeral; he had allowed himself to forget all about it. He goes to the window and wipes away their breath. The vicar, swaddled in his snowsuit, a can of petrol in one hand and Bible clutched to his chest in the other, is crossing the snow.

They dress in silence, shrugging on their snowsuits in the hallway and clipping on their snowshoes outside. The bells have called everyone from their houses. They join the flow of people crossing the ice from the quay to the pyre, the curls of their breath merging with the crowd.

Joe spots Alfie, his mum leaning on his arm for support. He spots Reg, muttering and red-faced; the two grockles from this morning, watchful and excited. It's a motley procession.

When they are halfway to the pyre the bells stop. The generator has been silenced and the eerie quiet is punctuated only by the shuffle-skitter of the top snow and rustle of nylon. What is it about a funeral, Joe thinks, that makes him want to burst out laughing?

He turns and looks back towards the quay and spots Alan and Sandra. Everyone else is keeping a respectful distance. They are grey-faced, practically reeling across the snow. Every now and then someone crosses the invisible cordon that has been drawn around them, to press hands and mutter a few words.

The crowd forms a loose circle around the pyre as they arrive, one by one. This is the second funeral they have held this way. Protocol, now established, comes as a relief. The first time they built a pyre on the river it was for an old woman who had lived alone by the Co-op and had died and frozen in her bed. Joe would have recognised her well enough to say hello in the street – always pulling that same tartan shopping cart – but not to know her name or her circumstances. There was a pattern, at the beginning, people falling through the gaps that were opening up in their community. Joe had been one of those who volunteered to help dig the grave, but the ice was too thick. They'd had to find another way.

Joe spent the whole service worrying that the pyre would melt a hole in the ice and plunge the whole village into the water below. He knew it was thick; one of the first things that he and Alfie had done once the river ice turned clear was to bore holes in order to try their hand at a bit of ice fishing. They'd watched some videos on their phones at the Nottage, but never had any luck. Another failed scheme. Or, perhaps not. The ice held.

But that wasn't the first time they had burned a body. The first time, there was no funeral.

The wind has picked up. People begin to shuffle, stamping their feet. The vicar has to raise his voice to make himself heard. He recites a prayer on forgiveness as the wind tugs at the tarpaulin. Joe finds that he can't focus on the words, and his eyes keep wandering to the plastic can of petrol that the vicar has placed at the foot of the pyre. An occasional choked sob is carried to him – Sandra – but Joe can't bear to turn and look. When the vicar has finished, he clasps his hands together and looks around expectantly, to see if anyone wants to add any words of their own. Joe joins with everyone present in averting his eyes and studying his feet, feeling that perhaps it wouldn't be such a bad thing if the flames did sear a hole in the ice and the river swallowed them all up.

They had found the guy at the Nottage. He was opening up with Alfie. They were laughing and joking and whatever, completely relaxed. Joe was about to go upstairs to check on the still when he jumped out. They must have startled him, and he panicked. Joe isn't sure, it all happened so fast. All he remembers is that the guy was on top of him, there was a sickening thud, and then the guy went slack, his head lolling unnaturally over Joe's raised arms. He looked up at Alfie, ashen-faced, holding an oar in his hand.

The vicar starts up again. 'Though I walk through the valley of the shadow of death, I will fear no evil; for you are with me.'

Alan steps forward, pulling something from the pocket of his snowsuit and placing it on top of the tarpaulin. He steps back – it's a battered, scruffy cuddly toy. More restiveness from the crowd, all too much to bear. Would it have been worse, in the church? Under the glare of the garish painted faces of the dead aldermen, under the gaze of Christ in carved wood? He thinks of the determination on the vicar's face as the pews were broken apart for firewood, at his direction, when they realised no one else could be laid to rest in the churchyard. The vaulted, stone void that was left afterwards. There's a certain measured solemnity in the way a cough echoes in the eaves of the church; something is preserved, but outside, in the chilled air . . .

The guy was skin and bones. The oar had broken his neck with a single blow. Who knows where he had come from. He was young. Joe had only seen his face for a moment, but he remembers every detail, the rage and fear in his eyes as he bore down on him, the tendons standing out in his neck. Without another word, they checked the rest of the building, but he was alone. They found the window that he had broken, in the first-floor toilet, and cleared away the glass. The vicar arrived as they were wrapping the body. Once they explained to him what had happened, he just kept grasping them by the shoulders in turn and repeating, 'It was an accident, he's with God now.' He spoke a few rushed words over the body and bade them take it away before anyone else could see it; such an accident shouldn't disrupt the fragile harmony, he said.

Alan speaks. Joe hears only the bitter flatness of his voice. He catches a few words when the wind drops. Robbed. Vicious. Forever. He feels eyes on his back and wishes that there had been time to build a coffin; he wishes that they had thought to wrap him in something other than plastic.

When Alan returns to Sandra's side the vicar steps forward. He picks up the can, fumbling at the cap with his mittened fingers, before circling the pyre and dousing it with the petrol.

'With this water we call to mind Ian's baptism.' The vicar's voice becomes more tremulous, as he warms to his theme. 'As Christ went through the deep waters of death for us, so may he bring us to the fullness of resurrection with Ian and all the redeemed.'

It was an accident. It was that terrible instinct, survival. But what happened next: the secrecy, the clandestine way in which they burned the body at the edge of the woods after dark was the seed of a sickness. An enclosure. One which was made only worse when the old lady died, and they tried to atone for that anonymous young man's death by making a spectacle out of hers. Bringing the village together, and burning her out on the river, had only underlined the fact that she died within the community, and he had died without.

Alfie steps up, holding a stick with a rag tied around the top. The vicar empties the last drops from the can onto the rag and Alfie lights it. He holds it out to Alan who draws back into himself a fraction, looking as though he might refuse it. But he steels himself and takes the torch.

'Goodbye, lad.'

He drops it at one corner of the pyre and turns, without another look, back to Sandra, wrapping her in his arms.

They haven't spoken of it since the first funeral: Joe holds it in silence, with Alfie and the vicar. They won't speak of it again. But all day he has been pushing a thought away. He always assumed that their accident had been the only one, but perhaps there have been others. Why else was Patrick allowed to walk away? Why else this reluctance to be the one to cast the first stone?

The wind drops. Joe closes his eyes against Sandra's low keening, muffled by Alan's snowsuit. It looks, for a moment, like the torch has gone out, but then the wind lifts and the flame licks its way along the rivulets of petrol; in an instant the tributaries converge and there is a roaring insuck of oxygen – a collective sigh of breath – as the plastic cracks, pops and the pyre is sheathed in flame.

HELEN

'That's that, then. There you have it.'

There is a certain satisfaction saying these words aloud, alone in the kitchen. She used to look forward to these moments: leafing through the *Gazette* after tea.

She would like to read a book, but the thought of getting up to find one is exhausting. If she had a book, she might be able to consider eating the fresh piece of cake that Bill cut and placed in front of her when the bells started up, before he went up to check on the bags. To spend a quiet hour at the bookshop, browsing the shelves, walking home with a crisp paper bag under her arm. She feels as though she should be infected with the same restlessness as Bill, but the exhaustion of the day has pressed her into a kind of contentment.

She pinches the back of her hand and watches the ridge of skin slowly collapse. She wants to run her hand over every surface in the kitchen, take out every pot and pan and ground herself in the freight of their use and misuse. To anoint them with her leaving.

It was when she first noticed that she couldn't focus on reading that she realised that something serious was off. She could take the words in, but they would be immediately displaced by the ones that followed. Like walking through the fine mist of a cloud.

There is a circular black scar on the table top, just next to the plate, where David stubbed out a cigarette. A response to some imagined sleight: one of those arguments born out of the tyranny of a twisted emotional logic that only surfaced when he was hammered. The ground on which they fought would continually shift under her feet; he wouldn't even allow her a right way of being wrong. She would apologise for neglecting him for one thing and then find this apology flung back in her face as evidence of some other form of neglect. She wants to go back and shake herself for being so biddable, for martyring herself at the altar of his crappy art. But what does it matter now.

The last time she saw him, from across the street in town, her first thought was that he had come to look as he had looked while sleeping: slack and somehow more innocent. All the way home she avoided shop windows and car mirrors and then sat down at her dressing table to stare at her reflection.

The kitchen is in shadow now; the sun has moved over to the front of the house. The weather has been unusually good today. They will need to leave soon or it will be dark.

The thought brings her to her feet. She gathers up the mugs and plates and takes them over to the sink. She wants an apple. She wants a crumpet, dripping with butter. A strobing numbness rolls up and down her right arm. She wants to cry. She can feel the force of the cold from the window above the sink. She wants to crack it open and smoke a cigarette, to let the smells of an evening meal escape. She wants to be met with the scent of the honeysuckle that Bill trained up the brickwork, to hear people laughing and chatting over the back wall in the pub garden. She wants to go to Southend for the day and play on the penny arcades. She wants to ride the stupid train down the pier to stare back at the lights and the rollercoaster; to taste the salt on her lips and get giddy at the beautiful, pointless fragility of being suspended on some matchsticks a mile out to sea. She wants to take every piece of china from the cupboard and smash them on the tiles one by one and leave the house and go to the pub and drink a pint of wine and never come back.

She leans on the sink to catch her breath. The steel is cool under her hands. She has a hard knot of frustration in her chest, the kind you have after you win an argument but are left with the greater injury. The snow and ice obscure all but the top part of the window and the little garden is completely smudged out. She is right to leave. It won't be long until it extends its fingers into the house to gather up the pots and pans, the mugs and plates, to strip them of their gentle glamour.

She sits down again and forces herself to eat some of the cake which recalls church fairs and school fetes: donating Joe's old toys only for him to buy them back with his clutch of hot pound coins.

She feels the tension of the funeral, taking place only a few hundred yards away, held between them. She takes a gulp of cold tea and the powdered milk cloys at the back of her throat. Bill sits down at the table opposite her, church-steepling his hands.

'They just lit the pyre. I watched the whole thing from the bedroom window.'

'Did you see Joe, and Rachel?'

'They were there. Almost the whole village were there. I

didn't know there were so many of us left. Can't think of the last time I saw so many together, in the same place.'

I should have been there, for Sandra, she thinks. But in truth she knows that the only person's pain she would be able to lessen would be her own.

'It will be strange to leave without saying any good-byes,' she says.

Bill's head turns and a moment later she twigs it: the generator, started up again.

'They'll all be at the Nottage soon,' he says. 'The wake.'

The front door goes. That'll be Joe and Rachel. One scenario that she has played out is that she waits until Bill, Patrick and Naomi are waiting at the front door, and Joe and Rachel are gathered on the stairs. As they are shrugging on their snowsuits she would slip upstairs and get her backpack, and, as they say their goodbyes, join the departing crowd with a small shrug of her shoulders, saying: that's that then, this is me. Very cinematic, sure, but she isn't some outlaw hitting the trail to go out in a blaze of glory. Can't put it off any longer, time to tell them.

'Dad?' Patrick is outlined in the doorway.

'Son? What are you ...' Bill tries to find words as he gets to his feet, taking bags from his son's hands. 'The funeral has only just—'

Patrick cuts him off. 'The halftracks. We heard them round the creek. We couldn't wait any longer. They're almost here.'

'That's that, then.' Helen levers herself up onto her feet using the table and circles the burn mark from David's cigarette with her index finger for luck, or something like it.

JOE

'We should show our faces,' Joe says.

'Should we?' says Rachel. They are walking back over the ice towards the Nottage. 'Isn't that what we just did?'

A lad nods to Joe; he was a couple of years above at school, they would sometimes walk to the bus stop together. Joe feels emboldened by this gesture of tacit support.

'We can't hide. We didn't do anything wrong.' The young man's slack, stricken face comes back to him again. Not a lie, not entirely true. 'And we have to live here. We have to show we're not ashamed to show our faces.'

Joe spots Alfie up ahead, walking with his mum. He turns and starts to move off towards him, he cannot wait to tell him about the baby. He forces all other thoughts aside. Rachel catches his hand and pulls him back. They stand aside as the crowd flows past. Joe feels conspicuous. He gives Rachel an enquiring look, but she casts her eyes down at the snow. The heat of the pyre is at his back. He resists the urge to turn and watch the flames.

She waits until the last stragglers are out of earshot. 'We can't stay here, Joe.'

'What do you mean, we can't stay here?'

'We can't raise a child in a house half-buried in the bloody snow.'

She sighs. He resents her for making him resent himself for making her state the obvious. He knows all this. He knows that, by the end of the argument, he will agree with her. But the argument has to be had anyway.

'Rachel, listen.'

'With no electricity, no running water. How could anyone—'

Joe interrupts her. 'What about Mum?'

She flinches and he turns away. It's as though she has just pulled a splinter from his thumb.

'This is what . . .' She throws her arms up in the air in frustration. He looks ahead, to the crowd, but no one turns. 'This what I have been trying to say. All day. All week. Been trying to build towards, for months. She can't stay here either! Did you think she would stay? Did you consider what Patrick leaving might mean for the rest of us? You need to wake up.'

He needs to be coaxed. The moment that he agrees that his mother is too ill to carry on here he is giving in to the fact that she's not going to get better. When he really thinks about it, he realises he has believed that she can't die if he doesn't accept that she is ill. Magical thinking.

'I forgot to ask; did you manage to get through to your mum earlier?' He still can't help but try to change the subject, buy himself some more time.

'Yeh.'

'Did you tell her about Patrick? About what he did?'

'No.'

'No – yeh, of course. Sorry, I don't know why I asked.' His stalling has thrown the conversation off track, and he's not quite sure how to find his way back.

'I didn't exactly want to follow the news that we're expecting her first grandchild with that.'

'No, no. Of course not.'

'Didn't exactly feel like the most natural moment to reveal that I'm living under the same roof as a murderer.' He flinches at the word, and hopes she doesn't notice – thinks she doesn't notice. Her eyes are focused on her snowshoe; she is flicking at the powder, sending small clouds up into the air. 'Thought it might dampen her excitement, you know?'

'No.' He pauses, wondering where to go next, knowing the way the conversation must end.

'I mean, how exactly do you imagine that segue playing out?'

'Look, it's hardly fucking surprising, is it, that it might be on my mind when . . .' He trails off and gestures back towards the burning pyre. And now they're fighting. It's his fault, trying to avoid talking about his mum. He knows he has no right to be angry, to play the injured party. But he can't help himself.

Rachel stops, and takes him by the arm. 'I do think it is surprising, yes. Pretty fucking surprising that your main worry is whether we're putting a proper face on it – whether bloody *Reg* and all those crusty old pricks are going to feel like we've made penance.'

'Rachel, I'm sorry. These past couple of days . . . it's a lot to take in.'

'You think I wanted to tell you like this? For it to be some footnote in this fucking psychodrama of male pain and pride? To bicker about it at a funeral.'

'You're right.' He takes her hands, turns her towards him, searching out her eyes. 'Look – you're right. You're right, you're right. We need to leave. All of us. We should go today.'

'We will go with the halftracks. They'll take me, if I tell them . . .' Her words dry up. He is sorry that he can't stop their unborn child from becoming a bargaining chip – a ticket out. 'And they'll take your mum, when they see her.'

Joe takes a deep breath. 'They will.' He pulls Rachel towards him and wraps her in his arms, her nose wet against his chin. He thinks of his mum in the sled this morning, wonders how he has managed to blind himself to the changes, and feels suddenly grateful to Rachel for not forcing him to look, for her patience in allowing him the chance to see for himself.

How much longer might things have gone on this way? It isn't the snow that stopped time but the isolation – spending each day with the same people has meant that he has no longer had to see himself, see his home or his family, through the eyes of others.

'I wonder what we'll remember, of this last year.'

'Hopefully, not too much,' Rachel says.

The acrid smell of burning plastic is brought to Joe on the wind and he shivers.

'Come on,' Rachel says. 'You're right, we should show our faces. If it is going to be for the last time.' She leads him across the ice.

The warmth hits Joe like a wave as soon as they come through the door to the Nottage. Everyone is standing with their snowsuits unzipped to their waists, rosy cheeked from the exposure. There is a palpable lull in the conversation as heads turn to take in their entrance. Alan, with his back to the door, surrounded by well-wishers, is oblivious. Sandra is nowhere to be seen.

The vicar makes a beeline in their direction, intercepting them near the door.

124

'Lovely service, Vicar.'

'Always difficult,' he says, 'finding the right words. Never more so than today, though, have to say.' He moves a little closer, inclining his head. 'Might want to give Alan a wide berth.' The vicar pauses, his mouth pursing in obvious frustration. 'I think Reg must have dropped a bottle around this afternoon, and he's a little the worse for it.'

'Where is Sandra?' Rachel says.

'She was inconsolable, she's been taken home.'

Joe is glad that they persuaded his mum to stay away. They wouldn't have been able to stop her following Sandra, which would have benefited no one. Reg totters over with a jug.

'Alreet, lad. Come to pour one out for the sorry bastard then, is it?'

'Alright, Reg,' Joe says.

'Terrible loss. Terrible shame. Young lad tha were so loved by so many.'

As Reg witters on, Joe is tempted to remind him what he said about Ian this morning, but he knows, from hard-won experience, that pointing out any contradiction in Reg's thinking simply makes him double down, heaping on outraged indignation. Joe decides it's better just to weather the platitudes.

When he has satisfied his piety, Reg hands Joe a mug and pours out some shine. He offers one to Rachel but she demurs, and the vicar places his hand palm down over his own to prevent Reg from topping him up.

Reg sidles off and Joe takes the opportunity to guide Rachel and the vicar away from the door and over to the wall, in an effort to make them less conspicuous.

'And, your brother?' the vicar says.

'Mum and Bill went to see him and Naomi. They spent the night out at Bowyer's farm.'

'Must have been freezing. Months now, since the Bowyers went.'

'Patrick is leaving. Not sure exactly when. But, he's going.'

'I'm glad. It's a shame, but I have to say I'm glad.'

A lot seems to have changed since this morning; he's starting to question whether he dreamed the conversations he had. Perhaps it was divine judgement that the vicar was referring to, when he said that Patrick would have to answer for what he had done. It's easy to forget that it's his remit, given that the primary topic of conversation of late has been the preservation of potatoes, or the distribution of fuel. Or perhaps he has just realised that there is no other authority left to intervene.

'We're leaving too,' Rachel says.

The vicar steps back, laying a hand on Rachel's sleeve. His head darting back and forth between them. 'You mustn't blame yourselves. And neither shall anyone else. If they do, I'll soon set them straight.'

'No,' Rachel says. 'Listen, it's not ...'

The vicar ploughs on: 'And I hardly think that just upping and leaving is ...'

But at that moment the sound of metal striking porcelain stops the vicar in his tracks. They turn to see Alan, standing on top of an overturned dinghy, striking the side of his mug with his fork. He is swaying from side to side and several people are reaching up at him, trying to coax him down, but he swats them away. The room falls silent.

'I just wanted to thank you all— ' He breaks off with a sob, one hand balled into a fist and held in front of his clenched teeth.

'My boy . . . I want to thank you all for coming to say goodbye.'
He takes a deep breath – determined. 'But I also wanted to say
that something needs to be done. He was murdered. In front of
the whole village, he was murdered. And . . .'

There are shouts of approval from the back of the room –
Reg's voice and a couple of others. The vicar calling Alan's name,
making his way towards him, soothing, cajoling.

Alan shouts over him, jeers rising from the crowd. 'And that
bastard has got to pay for what he's done!'

The door opens. Two men enter, wearing high vis over their
snowsuits, brushing snow from their shoulders and sleeves.
They remove the goggles obscuring their faces, eyes wide as
they take in the crowd and Alan at the centre.

One of the men holds a clipboard in his hands. He looks down
at it, and then back at Alan, a small frown creasing his brow,
as though he is inventorying the scene in front of him and has
concluded that something has fallen short.

The halftracks.

'This the Nottage? Wivenhoe?' the man with the clipboard
says. Joe realises he doesn't recognise either of the men from
previous runs.

The vicar steps forward. 'Yes.'

'I hope we're not interrupting something; we saw the fire out
on the river.' He pauses, waving the clipboard officiously. 'Could
you give us a hand with these boxes?'

HELEN

Helen picks up the rucksack that Bill packed for her from its place by the door of their bedroom and empties it onto the bed, to find out which items he defines her by.

When Naomi and Patrick said they were going up to pack, she felt inspired to do the same. Although it's hard to read anything into the assortment of faded knickers and tops that he has chosen to ball up in the bag. She lays them all out, one by one, and marvels at how washed out and threadbare they are.

She opens her drawers and starts pulling out clothes and dumping them onto the bed on top of the ones from the bag. She pulls off her leggings and tosses them into the corner of the room. She needs to plan outfits. She has to be efficient. She pulls on a pair of old stonewashed 501s but as she gets them over her bum it's immediately clear that there is no way that she will be able to button them up. It's enough to make her cry and she lies back on the bed with the jeans around her knees, hugging jumpers and tops that smell of stale lavender and mothballs to her chest. To think of all the years she has spent fighting those bastards. The tears turn to laughter and she squeezes the rough cotton between her fingers.

Bill is staring up at the ceiling with his arms crossed across his chest; a great leader lying in state. She imagines placing two pennies on his eyes and lighting a circle of candles. Before she had Joe she used to daydream about her funeral all the time. It was her favourite guilty pleasure, in idle moments when driving or doing the washing up: thinking about who would be there, who would give a eulogy, who would be the most gothic weeper, which of her friends who she had fallen out of touch with would profess too close a connection and make her family uncomfortable by getting really hammered at the football club after. But this game became too painful when Joe came along. To imagine his cherubic little face peeping over the front pew stuck a stake through her heart. Since the snow her preferred daydream has been to imagine the very thing that used to put her in that untethered state: driving a car. She pictures each turn that would take her from her house out of the village, past the university and towards town; checking her mirrors, indicating, and turning the wheel hand-over-hand with exaggerated slowness as she navigates the empty roads in the early morning light. There is something that she wanted to pack, if only she could remember what it is.

'Everything OK?' he says. 'You're looking at me like you might eat me.'

The front door opens and closes; Bill sits up.

'Mum!' Joe shouts up.

So, the time to tell him she is leaving has arrived – can be avoided no longer. It occurs to her that, had the snow not started to fall, had the hospitals stayed open, had she visited Dr Hope when the pains – the vagueness – first started, had she been poked and prodded and sat down in an anonymous office to be read her prognosis while Bill wrung his hands, she might have had a different conversation, sat next to her adult son on his childhood bed. She might have had this other conversation somewhere else, somewhere like a garden centre, ensconced in the gentle hum of anonymity surrounded by laughing Buddhas and gnomes and sacks of tea lights; she might have worn a summer dress, she might have rehearsed what she was going to say in front of a mirror, she might have had a packet of tissues in the front pocket of her bag. She would have found a way of saying *I'm leaving* which meant *I love you*. But either way the thrust of it would have been the same: the path is splitting. I have to go one way and you have to go the other.

'Mum?' He is roaming from room to room below, calling for her as he has a thousand times before. 'Where are you?'

There might be gentler ways for this to happen: children who leave home to go to university and who drift into separate, parallel lives, lived at the other end of a phone line. She hadn't felt that way when her mum had told her she had cancer. She hadn't felt any kind of distance. She was complaining about one of David's periods of weaponised silent withdrawal when her mum had tossed the news like a hand-grenade into the middle of her tirade. She asked all of the obvious questions, mechanically, but it suddenly seemed as though she was watching herself through the wrong end of a telescope. Breast cancer, stage two, surgery, radiotherapy ... the answers barely registered, and all she could feel was a sense of mild unfairness at the way the news had been sprung on her at the very moment she was demonstrating her least generous, least understanding qualities. As though her mum's cancer was a kind of rebuke to her whole character. It was a sense that she couldn't shake

130

until the final days of the cancer, when she no longer seemed like her mum at all.

She doesn't blame her for the way that she broke the news, because she can now feel the way that the pressure of it grows inside of you; a balloon leaning into a pin to let the pressure out.

'Mum!'

'Coming!' No putting it off, not a moment more. She pats her pockets, pats her chest, feels as though she has forgotten something. She fingers the St Christopher hanging around her neck.

Joe is waiting at the foot of the stairs.

'We need to have a talk.'

She nods. She can read on his face just how painfully slow her progress down the stairs is. It was cold in the bedroom; it's got into her joints. He places one hand on her shoulder and the other below her elbow as he guides her down the hall into the kitchen.

Rachel is sitting at the table. She sits down opposite. Joe looks at Rachel, then turns back to her and opens his mouth to speak.

'Joe,' she says, 'I'm leaving.'

She pauses. Joe's mouth still hangs wide and an array of emotions kaleidoscope across his face: shock preceding hurt – just as it had when he was a toddler in that instant after he had fallen over, before the report of pain had travelled back along his nerves from his brain – but rather than ending in tears, a sad smile forms on his face.

Helen isn't able to take this in, to consider what it might mean, so she presses on: 'I'm leaving, today, with the halftracks. Bill will be following Patrick.'

Rachel reaches out a hand across the table and Joe takes it in his.

'That's what I wanted to . . .' Joe says, trailing off. Trying again: 'We're leaving too. We're all leaving. And the halftracks are here.'

'You're leaving the village?'

'They arrived about fifteen minutes ago, we need to hurry.'

'You're coming with us?'

'They'll want to eat, which will take maybe another half an hour. Leaves us just over an hour.' Joe's eyes are scanning the room, unseeing; he wipes a hand over his mouth. 'We need to pack.' He stands.

Helen gawps at him. The anxiety of the day, building to this moment, now washes over her. She feels spent.

Rachel squeezes Joe's hand, nods to his seat. 'Helen, there is one more thing we want to tell you about.'

Joe nods, smiling. Excited now. What's going on? He sits, but he's leaning forward out of his chair. There is a roar, blood rushing in her ears, which makes it difficult to hear what is being said. She tastes metal on her tongue. Worked herself into a bloody lather for nothing. She watches Rachel's lips as she speaks. A baby. She said ... did she say a baby? They are out of their chairs, folding her in their arms. How long have they known? Have they been keeping the news from her? She needs to make some sound, to speak her gratitude, but she finds she cannot. She hopes that her tears are eloquent enough.

Rachel and Joe leave her. To pack? She watches the shadows lengthen over the surface of the table in front of her, the grain marking time. She wants to be close to the ground. She struggles up onto her feet and eases herself down onto a pile of bags that Bill has left, ready to be strapped to the sled.

She feels as she did as a child, when she woke early on the mornings of their family holidays, waiting for her parents to get out of bed. It is precious, suspended time, when – rather than waiting for the world – the world seems to be waiting for you.

Now that she has learned that she won't be losing Joe, she feels as though she can lift the veil she had draped over her future. If only by one corner.

All of the things that she had been so eager to abandon, every useless, worn-out artefact of her life, now seems precious. She wants to keep all of them. She wants to build a caravan of piled furniture, clothes, pictures, rugs, pots, pans, plates – all pulled by a horse-drawn cart like a family in a costume drama fleeing war. She would like to get Joe's baby clothes down from the loft. She hopes they are not too moth-eaten, the little cardigans and bootees knitted by forgotten friends and now-dead great-aunties.

What's going to happen to all of those ziplocked bags of charity shop loot in the attic, all of her summer dresses and jackets? What if Joe has a daughter? Now that there is a possibility that someone might have a use for them, that she might be able to pass them down, she feels the loss of them for the first time. Still, this is all secondary to her relief that they will all be together.

Rachel has appeared at her elbow, a backpack over each shoulder. She drops them on the floor next to the others and Helen reaches out to take her hand, drawing her to her side.

'I can still smell those currants. Lovely smell to carry out of the house with us when we leave.'

'How are you feeling?'

'I'm feeling OK, actually. Not too much pain. Is there any of that cake left?'

'I think so.' Rachel pats her hand and goes over to the stove to investigate.

Helen is unsure of the rules of her new role, as mother-in-law, as grandma-in-waiting, but she senses they are slightly different from before. Would she have reached out for Rachel's hand before today? She thinks probably not. The news has freed up her aspect towards her, which ossified somewhere in Joe and Rachel's teenage years; she held herself at a certain distance which she felt implied some vague defence of propriety, as though withholding herself from Rachel suggested that Rachel should withhold herself from Joe. Not that she really cared what they did, but she carried a congenital puritan strain which meant she would have been horrified to have to acknowledge it; admitting any closeness to Rachel would have implied a recognition of her closeness to Joe in turn. The news of the baby sweeps away all this nonsense – the pomposity of which she was aware, and which irked her, but not quite enough to shake her free – and admits the possibility that they might be more of a comfort to one another. It makes keener the guilt she feels for failing to address Rachel's separation from her mum more often. When her own mum had died, she felt something like homesickness. It took her some time to identify the feeling because she hadn't gone anywhere.

'I think I am quite unwell, Rachel.'

This is not what she expected to come out when she cleared her throat and opened her mouth to speak. She can't trust her thoughts from one moment to the next. The pain and exhaustion have robbed her of the old strategies by which she would reorder them, that allowed her to evade reckless impulses by getting up and moving around the room, wiping down surfaces and putting away cups. Rachel is halfway between the cooker and the table. She pauses midstride, a slice of cake held out in front of her like a retort. But then she closes the space between them in one step and puts a hand on Helen's arm. Her plaited ponytail falls across her chest and this, combined with the faded smock top she is wearing along with a sad, understanding smile, makes her seem otherworldly: like an Amish woman – some person from the past trapped in the future.

'I know. It's OK.'

She is stupidly grateful that Rachel didn't shield herself with misapprehension. It's such a relief. Bill and Joe are just protecting themselves with their insistence that everything is going to be OK and that the pain will pass, but to have your experience denied to you over and over, you can't help but start to wonder whether you are going mad.

'How are you feeling about it all?' Helen says.

'About the baby?'

'Yes.'

Rachel takes a breath but stops, considering her for a moment. She pulls a chair away from the table and sits across from Helen.

'It's OK,' Helen says. 'You can talk to me. Likelihood is I'll forget anyway and we can do it again tomorrow.' She laughs, with a little too much bitterness.

'I feel lots of things. Mostly I feel terrified.'

'Sounds about right. That's how I felt. And obviously excited. But in a way that was inseparable and almost indistinguishable from the terror.'

'I'll be glad to get away from this place in any case.'

'I couldn't agree more.' Helen turns, following Rachel's gaze over her shoulder to find Naomi standing in the doorway with her backpack in her hand. It seems as though people no longer enter rooms, they simply materialise.

Naomi sits on the edge of the table and starts rummaging around in her bag. 'Did I interrupt something?'

'No, don't worry, just chatting,' says Rachel.

'Every room I walk into seems to fall silent.'

'We were just talking about how we're all coming along now.'

'Where's Patrick?' Helen says.

'Upstairs. Sleeping, perhaps. Making himself scarce, for all the good it will do us now. Little bit late. I was just praying that there would be one last cigarette in here that I somehow forgot about. Heaven knows I've checked a hundred times already.' She closes her rucksack with a violent tug. 'Did you say everyone is coming along?'

'Joe and I . . .' Rachel falters, looking over towards Helen for encouragement. She remembers this part, having to speak the news in order to take ownership of it, to test the evidence of your body against the reactions of your loved ones. She was grateful to Rachel for acknowledging her pain and now she's grateful, once again, that she has made her a party to this pleasure. She nods her head and smiles.

'I'm pregnant. My period is late.'

'Oh my god.'

'So that's why we're leaving.'

'Oh my god.'

Naomi drops her bag on the floor and closes her arms around Rachel, shrieking, and hanging on as though she is a life raft. Helen realises that she is laughing too. Her nerves are ringing with something other than pain and she hasn't been this present all day.

'It's a good thing you are coming with us,' Naomi says, pulling away, solemn. 'It's no place to raise a child, here.'

It's amazing how living with pain makes you so alive to every feeling, like your skin has opened, offering your nerves up to the air. Naomi must feel it too, the wind's every breath. Every snowflake alighting on the delicate hair of her neck.

'It will be like the coach ... that Gifted and Talented trip,' Rachel says. 'Year eight, was it?'

'Except maybe you'll let me sit with you this time,' Naomi says with a laugh, folding her knuckles under the curve of her jaw, 'without those bitches from the year above around to impress.'

Rachel pushes Naomi playfully, and then folds her into a hug once more.

When Rachel releases her, Helen takes Naomi's hand, and takes Rachel's with her other, pulling them towards her. Their hands are warm and limp; her palms are dry. She smiles at each in turn. It's awkward. It's a start.

JOE

The sun is huddled low now, the last flare of a fagend, but it's throwing a real carnival against the clouds as it burns out. Reds, purples, oranges – the whole business. A good sky to go out on. It will be dark by the time they get on the halftrack. That is, assuming that they are allowed on.

He wasted five minutes looking for his keys, before it occurred to him that he wasn't going to need them. Now he is staring out the window. He wonders how long it will be until someone moves in. Must pack. He is stuffing socks into a ruck-sack when Rachel comes in, handing him a slice of cake, and tucks into one of her own.

'Who knows when we'll next get a proper meal.'

'How's Mum doing?' Joe says.

'Exhausted,' Rachel says. 'But happy, I think. She seems happy.'

'The double take when you told her about the baby. Priceless.'

'Was pure vaudeville.'

They sit in silence for a moment, enjoying their cake.

'What do you think might have happened at the Nottage?' Joe asks. 'If the halftracks hadn't arrived?'

She stops chewing, picks at the currants, placing a couple of burnt ones on the dresser. 'I don't know, doesn't bear thinking about. But I expect we'll hear more of the same when we turn up with Patrick in tow.'

Joe sighs. 'And the rest.'

'Naomi is still convinced we're going to get killed.'

'Rachel, we've known these people all our lives.'

'No use in worrying about it now, in any case.' She pops the last bite of cake into her mouth.

A knock at the front door.

'That'll be Alfie,' he says. He zips up the bag and runs down the stairs with it. Shrugging his snowsuit up over his shoulders, he throws open the front door.

He is back at it, humming 'Winter Wonderland'. Alfie, standing at the gate, staring out at the setting sun. Joe joins him.

'They're done and dusted over at the Nottage then?'

'Can't fucking believe you're going to be a dad. You. Of all people.'

'Hate to break it to you, mate, but most people – in fact nearly all people – become dads.'

'Not me, mate, I'm a lone wolf.'

Joe follows Alfie's outstretched arm to where his finger points at the moon, full and pale, and rising behind them. Alfie drops his arm and throws back his head, howling up at the sky. Joe's first instinct is to laugh it off. But it's irresistible. He fills his chest with the cold air and howls at the moon alongside his friend, wringing his lungs of the tension of the day.

'Got to hand it to you, mate,' Alfie says, after they have caught their breath. 'You picked quite the moment to tell me. Strange news to break at a funeral.'

'I only found out myself today.'

Alfie clocks the backpack slung over his shoulder, and a moment of recognition passes over his face, as he puts two and two together. 'I guess you're leaving, then.'

'I guess we are,' Joe says. He waits for Alfie to say something more, and when he doesn't, Joe feels a pressing need to fill the silence. 'Do you remember when . . .'

'It's come to seem like remembering is all we do, mate.'

He was going to ask whether Alfie remembered the foreign languages day trip they took to France when they were in their first year of secondary school. They had been let off the bus to wander around a small anonymous town for an hour or so before driving back to the Tunnel. A whiny, slightly chubby boy named Rich had been following them around all day, and when he went into a shop to buy a drink, they ran away and abandoned him. They laughed hysterically all the way to the bus. When Rich eventually found his way back, he was crying, but was too embarrassed to admit that he had got lost because Joe and Alfie had run off on him. He sat at the front of the bus next to the teachers all the way home and didn't follow them around after that.

It was one of those formative, shameful adolescent experiences that they had shared, but never talked about. He is glad that he didn't bring it up. It's no kind of goodbye, dredged-up shame.

Patrick and Naomi emerge from the house, with Rachel and Bill behind, one arm under each of his mum's. Everyone gathers together in the middle of the street, bags strapped to one sled, Helen strapped to another. Her head is still bowed and she is holding their hands by the fingers at the second knuckle, which has something priestly about it.

'We all ready to go?'

'I think so,' says Bill, picking up the line to Helen's sled. Joe takes up the other.

'Well, we best get a move on, then.'

'Yeh, they'll be finished with their tea soon enough,' says Alfie. 'Let's go, I'll come along with you.'

Joe catches Rachel's eye and she smiles. It steadies him, makes him feel resolved.

They fall into single file and start to wind their way towards the Nottage. He already knows in his bones that as the baby grows Ian will recede until he is forgotten. Another faint outline in the snow.

HELEN

Entering the village from the direction of town, driving down the high street, there are cars parked on the left-hand side all the way down. Approaching the bottom end – past the Spar, past the Co-op – the road narrows, and it gets more and more difficult for two cars to pass, forcing those entering the village from town to pull over in the spaces between the parked cars. Right of way goes to those who are leaving, rather than those who are coming home.

Helen never had much patience for this arrangement. Every time she was forced to pull to the side, she felt a twinge of anger. Early one morning, driving home from work, as she approached the Co-op a bus parked at the bus stop suddenly accelerated and tried to force her over. Without feeling as though she had consciously made a decision, she decided to ignore the cue and drove on. The bus had already passed the first car in the line on her left-hand side, so there was no room to pass. The bus came to a standstill and she stopped, almost bumper to bumper. As she stared up at the bloated, rage-creased face of the driver, as he pushed his ridiculous wrap-around shades onto the top of his head, she felt a sense of utter serenity. My home, my right of way.

After ten seconds the driver started to gesticulate, and after twenty he leaned on the horn. Eventually he slid his window open and started yelling fucking cow fucking bitch what the fuck are you doing. That settled it. She picked up her thermos cup of instant coffee and got out of the car. She walked over to the driver's window and stood, basking in her cloud of serenity and sipping her coffee, as the bus driver yelled himself puce.

When he had tired himself out, and it became clear that she wasn't going to move, he slammed the window shut and backed the bus up. Helen climbed into her car and sailed past him, in her expensive delicate ship, as he convulsed with impotent rage.

Will she ever feel like that about a place again? Could anywhere else make her feel striped with rightness from head to toe? She always winced to be described as brave; it's always levelled with the freight of either tragedy or foolishness. Brave to have a child so young – oh, so stupid! – brave to make do without his father – oh, so sad! But the way she felt that day, the word couldn't have been wielded against her.

She can hear people shouting now but, just like that day, the words don't really register. She is warm and for the moment comfortable, wrapped in all the sleeping bags that Bill could find in the house.

She is full of the same certainty today. Whether another place might feel like home, or not, the time has come to leave. And as she feels herself pull free of that knot of guilt and shame, longing rushes in to fill the gap. She wants to watch rain comb the hills in the Lake District. She wants to dip her fingers into a tub of ice cream. She wants to swim in a sea so cold it makes her jaw hurt. She wants to pop grapes between her teeth in the sun trap in the front garden on the first warm day of spring in the peace of the late afternoon, just before air fills with the sound of kids laughing on their way home from school. Free of her fear of losing her home, of losing Joe, she is free to feel the loss of everything else.

'Are you OK?' Bill's face appears, framed by his hood. 'Won't be long now, we'll be able to rest.'

She must be crying; she can feel the pinch of the tears freezing on her cheeks. She puckers up and he leans down to kiss her.

As Bill pulls away, Joe's face comes into view, and then disappears. She wonders, idly, for a moment, how the two of them will get along without her. She feels optimistic.

The world drops and she sways. She throws out an arm and one side finds Bill, she throws out the other and finds Joe. As the hum of an engine fills her ears, a movement catches her eye – a prowling shape behind the massed people, white against the shadowed eaves.

JOE

'We want you to take us back with you. To the exit point.'

The hauler turns from the vicar, to whom he was handing a plate. He takes Joe in and then looks at each person in turn behind him, eyes finally landing on his mum lying half-asleep in the sled at Bill's feet. They must look like quite a motley crew.

The man shouts to make himself heard over the sound of the generator. 'Have a fuckin' laugh, mate. It's not a bus.'

He collects his clipboard, secures the stub of a pencil in the fold of his beanie hat.

Rachel steps forward.

'I'm pregnant.'

Joe feels the spectre of violence rear up as the man assesses her. He licks his cracked lips.

'Doctor's note?'

'There hasn't been a doctor through in two months now.'

He grunts. Naomi steps forward.

'I'm pregnant too.' She loops her arm through Rachel's and with this sisterly gesture the stink of sexual menace evaporates.

'All you pregnant?' He laughs, waving his pencil. 'You?' He points at Patrick. 'An' you?' He points at Joe.

'Come on,' says Rachel. 'You've got nothing left. The truck is empty. What's the harm?'

'You think there is room for everyone?' He nods to the crowd starting to gather in the doorway to the Nottage behind him, laying down cylinders of gas and rucksacks full of supplies that have just been unloaded. They shiver and stamp as they adjust to the cold after the heat of the Nottage; their breath steams as they fan out along the quayside. The place is on its last legs; why has it taken Joe until now to realise? The two grockles emerge, the older one shouldering a bag filled to the brim with tins. The younger one is no longer limping. Joe wonders whether they will stay, or whether they are just taking advantage of the sudden, temporary surplus. He eyes the younger one warily. He hopes that the older one will decide to temper his brother's curiosity as he did this morning.

Joe senses a rising murmur from the crowd. He turns to find Patrick at his elbow. For chrissake, they agreed that he would stay out of sight until Joe had negotiated with the drivers.

'Someone spotted me,' Patrick grunts in his ear. 'I'm not going to cower like a dog.'

Reg mutters darkly, a bottle of shine in one hand and a sack of potatoes at his feet. There was a moment, some point over the course of this afternoon, that Joe became complicit. He tried to see the scene through the haulers' eyes. Imagines himself in the pristine high-vis. He feels the gulf that has opened up between his present and former lives in the space of only a year.

The man with the clipboard folds his arms. 'What's all this about, anyway?'

The other hauler sighs with ostentatious impatience and climbs up into the cab of one of the two vehicles.

Joe waits, for someone to say something, challenging them. The whole village is ranged along the quay. He tries to meet their eyes, one by one: willing them to stay silent. There's something in the air. Not anger. Closer to a swelling disappointment. A stretched balloon that's too knackered to pop. This isn't the spectacle they hoped for, that they are freezing their bitter old bollocks off for. He is filled with a sudden fury that the fate of his unborn baby is now tied to the fortunes of his fool of a brother. Patrick is as silent as the muted onlookers. The tinder is there, he can tell that all it needs is a spark.

Joe is thinking to himself that he is grateful for how the rattling drone of the generator undercuts the silence, when Alan reels out of the door, almost careening head-first into the snow piled around the entranceway. The vicar catches his arm, and he rights himself. There is a subtle shift, as the attention of the people gathered collects around him.

Alan slowly takes in his surroundings. Absolutely hammered now, his capillaries a livid topography. The whole crowd follows his gaze, a single held breath, until they finally alight on Patrick.

He raises an arm, points to Patrick. His face creasing into a mask of hatred. 'Fucking. Murdering. Bastard.' Joe's only thought, as Alan spits the words out one by one, is that he hopes that Patrick doesn't flinch.

But as Alan speaks, there is murmuring from the crowd and Joe can feel its focus shift. He turns towards the sound and can't quite believe what he sees.

Down the quay, just outside the pub: a bear. Less than thirty yards away, a real-life polar bear. In profile, it is huge and dirty – jet-black skin visible underneath its patchy pale yellow fur. It tosses its head and paces back and forth, eyeing the crowd imperiously and impetuously.

Alan finally notices and gasps. He reels backwards, his momentum this time too great for the vicar to counter, and falls backwards, crashing into the powder before hitting the compacted snow below with a sickening thud.

No one pays him any mind. One by one, mobile phones are emerging from bags and snowsuits, all trained in one direction. Everyone is too mesmerised to panic. It is something that Joe hasn't seen in over a year, since before the snow: the moment a crowd becomes an eye. The villagers tourists in their home.

Joe has to act. He steps between the hauler with the clipboard and Alan, sprawled in the snow. This is the moment. 'Well,' he says. 'What do you say?'

The hauler is transfixed by the bear. 'How did it get so close . . .' It has neither advanced nor retreated, and continues to pace in impetuous circles by the pub. 'What do I say about what?'

'About us, taking us along with you.'

The hauler finally comes back to himself; he straightens up, considering Alan for a fleeting moment with a look that mingles pity and disgust, a look that Joe feels is as much for him – for the community – as it is for Alan himself. It is a look that doesn't consider the words that Alan has spoken, only the spectacle of his drunkenness and hostility that undermines them.

The blast of a horn cleaves the air; everyone jumps. The polar bear rears up onto its hind legs and roars. So close that Joe can see the strings of spittle matting the hair around its jaws. The crowd begins to break up, thinning out along the quay in the opposite direction. The bear turns in a circle and rears up again. For a moment it looks as though it might charge but then another blast brings it back onto all fours. It bellows as it turns tail, cantering across the river ice towards the opposite shore.

Joe can see the other hauler gesticulating in his cab. The man waves his clipboard back at his partner, casts a longing look at his own vehicle.

'She really pregnant?' He nods towards Rachel, but his face has set, his decision has been made. He wants to get out of here, with the minimum of friction and fuss. He just wants the opportunity to frame it as a kindness.

'She's pregnant,' Joe says and, for good measure, gesturing towards Helen, 'and my mum is sick.'

The man takes one last look at what remains of the gathered crowd. The vicar is helping Alan – who is sobbing now – slowly to his feet, attempting to bundle him back into the Nottage. It's a strange scene: some people are oddly calm, whereas others are in full flight. Joe catches Alfie's eye and twitches his head. Alfie nods, grimly, and goes to lend a hand. Joe supposes he was right – the vicar is happy to leave the judgement and punishment to God.

The hauler sighs. 'On with ya, before I change my mind.'

Joe reaches out and grasps the man by his elbow.

'Hope there's more like you along the way.'

'You'd be lucky to find a softer touch. Come on, mate.'

The hauler disappears around the other side of the truck and climbs into the driver's seat, tossing the clipboard beside him. Joe turns and nods to the others. They need to move quickly, before anything changes. The bear will be back, the crowd will re-form. Joe walks towards the others, back up the path of trampled snow that marks where the jetty had once been. A few forlorn masts still thrust upwards through the snow along the length of the quay, their rigging frozen in place. Another denuded woodland that Joe won't be sorry to leave behind. Patrick has unstrapped the packs from the sled. His hands are shaking. Together they sling them through the open hatch of the truck.

'You alright, mate?' Joe asks.

'Let's just get the fuck out of here.'

Patrick takes off a glove and his fingers fumble over the clips that bind his snowshoes to his boots. When he finally gets them off he knocks them against the caterpillar tracks and climbs in with the bags. As Joe takes Rachel's hand and helps her up into the truck he is reminded of the first time he took the little ferry that carried people across the river at weekends during the summer. He remembers being frustrated by wasps as he tried to eat an ice cream at the pub in the village that faced theirs, looking at his home across the water and feeling like his nose was pressed up against a fish bowl, his finger tapping the glass. A feeling he felt again the first time he saw a local artist's linocut print of the quay on the wall in the pub: there's that life I've been living, as far as anyone knows it. He feels it once more, for what he knows will be the last time, as he slaps his way up the compressed snow to Bill and his mum. The crowd has regathered, huddled around the door to the Nottage, ready to retreat to safety. None step forward. They know they have missed their chance.

'Is she ready, then?' Joe says.

'As she'll ever be. She was right about the bears, I'll never live it down,' says Bill.

'Do you want a hand?' says Alfie, walking up from the quay.

'Nah, you're alright.'

Joe kneels down and grasps the sled's runner. Helen sways slightly in the sled as he and Bill steady themselves, their careful synchronicity, and the leaden weight of her body as she rolls and settles sends a shudder abseiling down Joe's spine. But then he feels her hand on his wrist, her grip strong and steady, her fingers probing the space between bone and muscle.

They stagger towards the truck and hoist her into the doorway. Rachel and Naomi grab the sled and pull it in.

Joe turns to look back towards the village one last time. Alfie, stood slightly apart, raises an arm. With a rush of sadness, of fear, of nausea and – finally – of hope, he steps inside.

Acknowledgements

Firstly, thank you to Lucy, without whose love and support this book would never have been written. Thank you to my Dad and Liz for always being my first and best readers.

Thank you to Matthew Turner for his patience and structural vision. To James Gurbutt for his shared love of Essex and his editorial guidance, and to everyone at Corsair for their careful and generous attention.

Thank you to all the people who have read this book in all of its many versions: Antony Hurley, Dan Fuller, Jake Franklin, Luke Chattaway, Rowena Wallace and all of the REGENERATE crew. And to So Mayer whose insight, friendship and conversation continue to inform everything I do.

Thanks to the Author's Society for the grant which allowed me to take time away from the bookshop to write the first draft, and to Gabriel and Olivia for hosting me, keeping me company and keeping me sane while I did so.